ANCHORED INN

A GRAY WHALE INN MYSTERY

KAREN MACINERNEY

GRAY WHALE PRESS

Copyright © 2020 by Karen MacInerney

All rights reserved.

No part of this book may be reproduced in any form or by any electronic or mechanical means, including information storage and retrieval systems, without written permission from the author, except for the use of brief quotations in a book review.

This book is a work of fiction. Names, characters, places, and incidents are either products of the author's imagination or used fictitiously. Any resemblance to actual events or locales or persons, living or dead, is entirely coincidental.

Other books in the Gray Whale Inn Mysteries:

The Gray Whale Inn Mysteries

Murder on the Rocks

Dead and Berried

Murder Most Maine

Berried to the Hilt

Brush With Death

Death Runs Adrift

Whale of a Crime

Claws for Alarm

Scone Cold Dead

Anchored Inn

Cookbook: The Gray Whale Inn Kitchen

Four Seasons of Mystery (A Gray Whale Inn Collection)

Blueberry Blues (A Gray Whale Inn Short Story)

Pumpkin Pied (A Gray Whale Inn Short Story)

Iced Inn (A Gray Whale Inn Short Story)

Lupine Lies (A Gray Whale Inn Short Story)

1

It's not every day an eclectic, reclusive multimillionaire rents the entire upper floor of your inn. At least not if you run a small establishment in quaint Cranberry Island, Maine.

As my niece Gwen and I went over arrangements in the cozy yellow kitchen of the Gray Whale Inn, I started fretting over all the extra requests we'd agreed to in order to host Brandon Marks. He'd made his millions (or billions) with a social media platform called WhatsIn, and despite the "social" nature of his business, he was a notorious recluse. I had no idea how he was going to manage on an island with subpar Internet, but his staff hadn't asked or added anything about it to the rather extensive list, so I hoped they'd figure it out.

"Let's go over the checklist one more time," I said as Gwen looked over the list Brandon's assistant had sent me. Gwen had come to stay with me when I opened the inn, taking a break from her studies at UCLA to spend the summer helping out around the place while I launched the business. She'd begun painting under the auspices of the late Fernand LaChaise, and soon discovered she not only had a rare talent for watercolor, but a deep and abiding love for Cranberry Island——and for Adam Thrackton, the only Maine lobsterman I knew of to have earned a degree from Princeton.

Her mother, my sister Bridget, had been on board with the match until she figured out that Adam's work, while it did technically involve merchandise and a boat, was not in fact international shipping, but fishing. Family life had been rocky for a while, but things had finally calmed down between Bridget and Gwen, at least for the time being, and Gwen had recently started the Cranberry Island Art Guild, which provided classes for artists of all levels as well as gallery space. We'd been working together to set up some art retreats for the coming year, figuring it would boost both our businesses, and hoped to get the first promotional materials together before Christmas.

Having Gwen here at the inn was a real treat; she no longer lived above the kitchen, as she had for years, and now spent most of her days at the Art Guild, working on her own art, teaching classes, or managing the other artists. Now that it was fall, though, things were slowing down for the season, and with the sudden rush at the inn, she'd offered to help me out. My mother-in-law Catherine was pitching in, too; she'd headed to the mainland to pick up a few things Brandon's assistant had requested at the last moment and that were not readily available from the small store on the island. Gwen drew circles on the corner of the page and sighed. "I know he's gluten-free, but any other weird dietary restrictions?"

"No sugar, some dairy," I said.

"Ouch. That's a culinary challenge." She eyed the batter I

was putting together. "So is it safe to assume that coffee cake you're making is not for them?"

"Correct," I said. "It's for my other guests, Max and Ellie."

"I like them," Gwen said, a faint smile crossing her face.

"So do I," I said. The two women, Max Sayers and Ellie Cox, were from Boston; Ellie owned a bookstore, and Max was her assistant manager; they'd checked in a few days earlier. Evidently the trip to Cranberry Island was a post-divorce "cleansing" of sorts for Max, who had just parted ways with her husband of twenty years and was trying to figure out what to do with her life. Ellie had reserved rooms for both of them; evidently they'd become very close friends.

"I hope Max'll make it through okay; she seems nice, but shell-shocked."

"Oh, I think she will," I said. "Once she gets herself together, she'll bloom." I'd never divorced, but I'd been through a nasty break-up. It had taken a while for me to realize it, but it had been the best thing that ever happened to me. And if I hadn't gone through it, I never would have met my husband, John. I smiled just thinking about him; this morning he was down in his workshop doing a toy boat order for Island Artists. Christmas was right around the corner, so even though the inn business usually slowed down, things usually picked up in the workshop around this time of year. "Plus, she's a good egg; I can tell."

"Me too," Gwen said. "When's the bigshot coming in, by the way?"

"He's actually flying in via helicopter and then taking a private boat," I informed her. "They'll transport him directly to the dock."

She looked up at me, eyebrows practically up to her hairline. "You're joking, right?"

"Nope," I said.

"Oh, man. It's going to be like a reality show here the next few days, I'm afraid."

"You may be right," I said as I finished chopping up a few apples I'd picked from one of the many trees dotting the island. I had no idea what kind they were, but they were small, with russet and red skins, and both tart and firm, perfect for the cake I was making. "But it will help with the bank account," I reminded her as I added the apple chunks to the batter for the decadent apple-cinnamon coffee cake I was making for my non-gluten-free guests. Outside, the birch and maple trees were glowing gold and red, and the sky was a vivid blue; it was a beautiful late fall afternoon on Cranberry Island, and despite the slight worry over getting everything right for our soon-to-be-arriving finicky guest, I was feeling pretty good about life in general.

"All right, let's get through the rest of this, then. Organic detergent only on towels and sheets," my niece read, pulling her dark, curly hair up into an impromptu bun as she spoke.

"I rewashed everything and Catherine remade the bed in his room."

"Check, then. Gluten-free breakfast, coconut oil and stevia for coffee—do we have the brand of coffee he requested?"

"We do," I assured her. I'd had the special coffee (hand-picked by free-range, organically fed baboons? Roasted over seasoned mahogany? At 40 dollars a pound, I certainly hoped so) overnighted; it had come over on the mail boat from the mainland the day before. "And Catherine's picking up the organic coconut oil on the mainland today; she's visiting a friend for dinner and will be back with it tonight."

"Good," Gwen said, looking a little green around the gills as she finished tying up her hair and made a checkmark on her list. She glanced up at me, her face a pale oval under the mass of hair; she looked drawn, I noticed, and her black cardigan sweater seemed to hang on her thin frame. "They're paying extra for all this, right?"

"A lot extra, or there's no way I'd do this." Brandon had booked the entire upper floor, taking the biggest suite for himself and the adjacent rooms for his two assistants. The other rooms were to be left vacant, lest his majesty be disturbed. It must be nice to have that kind of cash to throw around, I thought as I finished mixing the batter and poured it into the baking pan.

"Why did they pick the island, anyway?" Gwen asked.

"Evidently he likes his privacy," I told her, scraping the bowl as I spoke. "I think he's landing his helicopter just up from the dock; he paid the island a few thousand dollars for the privilege. They're going to put it toward the museum, I heard."

"So Murray Selfridge is not going to be the wealthiest guy in town for a week or two," Gwen said, grinning.

I put down the bowl and reached for the brown sugar. "Not by a long shot. I heard the Jamesons and the Karstadts are also here for the summer." Both families were long-term summer residents of the island, but didn't mingle much with the rest of us, limiting their contact to the harbormaster (they had to moor their fancy boats somewhere, after all) and the folks who took care of maintenance issues for them. It wasn't ideal, but it did provide some work and funds for islanders.

"Where did he make all his money, anyway?"

"Social media," I said as I dumped brown sugar into a small bowl and then spooned flour into the same measuring cup. I added it to the sugar with some cinnamon and butter, and set to work cutting the butter in with a fork; I could almost taste the sweet, buttery streusel already, and forced myself to remember what we were talking about instead of fantasizing about coffee cake. I looked up at Gwen. "Brandon's company went public a few years ago, and now he's wealthy enough to buy a Central American country. Maybe more than one."

"Must be nice," she said.

"I think I'd rather live on Cranberry Island," I said, truthfully. Although with the discovery of a long-missing German U-Boat a few miles off the coast a week ago, things had suddenly gotten a bit crazy. Since the team funded by Brandon had identified the wreck, just about every person on the island with a Y-chromosome had suddenly discovered a deep, hidden passion for World War II naval ships. Apparently the U-Boat in question had destroyed at least a dozen ships, some of which had borne islanders' relatives, before disappearing; Brandon was on the island in order to observe the first trip to the U-Boat with a submersible, which was expected to definitively identify the vessel.

"This whole submarine thing is a pretty big deal, isn't it?" Gwen asked as she did a last check of the list. I might not be fascinated by it, but I was happy to be hosting the funder of the expedition that had located the U-Boat, and so was half the island.

As I sprinkled the streusel over the batter, I glanced over at my niece. The drawn look worried me. "Are you okay?" I asked.

"I'm just not feeling well these past few days," she said.

"I hope it's not flu," I said.

"Me too," she said, grimacing. "At least Adam hasn't caught it. There's supposed to be bad weather coming this weekend, too; I wish he'd stay home on blustery days, but he never does."

"Good work ethic cuts both ways, doesn't it?" I said as I tucked the cake into the oven.

"It does," she said. "At least he loves his work."

As she spoke, John walked through the back door into the kitchen, smelling of paint and that particularly woodsy smell that I found so intoxicating. A cool breeze accompanied him, bringing the scent of salt air and falling leaves.

"What's in the oven?" he asked, eyeing the bowl I was about to wash. He was wearing jeans and a green plaid flannel shirt that brought out the color of his eyes. Sawdust streaked his sandy hair, and there was a fleck of red paint on his cheek, which was absolutely adorable (although I didn't tell him).

"Apple coffee cake," I informed him.

"Gluten-free?"

"No," I said. "I made some strange almond flour concoction I found online earlier today, and we'll scramble some eggs and serve fruit salad in the morning."

"What about dinners?"

"Salmon and green beans, with sweet potato on the side and gluten-free bread from the mainland."

"Sounds like everything here is under control," he said. "I just finished painting the last batch of boats; once they dry, I'll take them to the store. I'm done in the workshop for the day, so I'm happy to take care of dinner."

"Thanks," I said, getting up on tiptoes to kiss him.

He gave me a kiss, which made me all warm inside, and accompanied it with a squeeze, then looked at Gwen. He tilted his head as he took in her wan face. "Are you okay? You don't look so hot."

"I'm just a little under the weather," she said.

I glanced at John. "She's just going over last-minute preparations. But since you're here, why don't you take that over so we can send her home to rest?"

"I'm fine," Gwen protested. "Really."

"I think we've got everything here under control," I said with more confidence than I felt. The smell of apple cake baking was beginning to permeate the kitchen; I took a deep breath of the apple-cinnamon scent, then said, "Gwen, I'm ordering you to take the rest of the afternoon off."

"Are you sure?" she asked, looking even greener than she had earlier.

"Absolutely," John told her. "Now, go home and rest."

"And take this container of chicken noodle soup with you," I said, opening the freezer and pulling out a plastic tub of soup I'd put in a few days earlier. "Do you have tea?'

"Yes, Mom," she said.

"You're welcome to curl up in your old room," I told her. "We can drive you back to the house when Adam's here."

"I... I..." She stood up suddenly, hand on her mouth, and ran up the stairs.

John and I looked at each other as she disappeared.

"I think it's best if she stayed here," I said, and put the soup back in the freezer.

"I'll leave Adam a message," John said. "And then I'll do a last check on the rooms and do the dinner prep."

"Have I mentioned recently how much I love you?"

"You have," he said with a grin, "but you know I always love to hear it again."

I was about to kiss him a second time when the phone rang.

I sighed and picked up the receiver. "Gray Whale Inn."

"Natalie? It's Charlene."

I could tell by her voice that something was very amiss with my best friend, who ran Cranberry Island's general store and post office. "What's going on?" I asked, gripping the phone.

"Tania's gone missing," she said.

2

"What do you mean, gone missing?" Tania was Charlene's beloved niece, and often helped her out at the store. She was around twenty years old, and still figuring herself out.

"She was supposed to be here this morning, but she never showed up. She sent me a quick text late last night to say something came up and she'd be out of touch for a bit. I've called and texted her a half a dozen times, but there's no answer."

"Maybe her phone's broken?" I suggested.

"No," Charlene insisted. "That's not like her. I have a bad, bad feeling about this."

"Did you call her best friend? Megan Canfield, right?" I asked.

"I did," she said. "Megan's not answering her phone. Can you come down and help me figure out what to do?"

"I'll be over shortly," I promised. "I'm sure she's fine." I put a confidence into my voice I didn't feel.

"Thank you so much," Charlene said, sounding relieved. "I'm probably overreacting, but... it's not like her."

"I get it," I said. "I'll be there as soon as I can."

"What's wrong?" John asked as I hung up the phone.

"Tania's missing," I told him. I reported what Charlene had told me. "She wants me to come down to the store and figure out what to do next." Charlene ran the grocery store/post office, also known as the island's living room; it was where everyone went to have a mug of tea and catch up on the local happenings, or just to pick up mail or a gallon of milk. "I'm thinking we need to go talk to her friend Megan in person, and see if she knows anything about Tania; she's not answering her phone."

"Do you think Megan has something to do with it?"

"I have no idea," I said. "How long before you can put out a missing persons report?" Since John was not just an artist and woodworker, but the island deputy, I figured he would know.

"She did say she'd be gone, so it's not like she totally disappeared, but I'll call the mainland police and ask about it," John said, looking concerned. As he spoke, here was a thrumming from behind the inn.

"What's that?" I asked, peering out the back window at the sweep of ocean and the craggy mountains of the mainland beyond.

"I think our special guest has arrived," John said just as I spotted a helicopter in the bright blue sky.

John and I hurried to the back deck, shielding our eyes against the bright afternoon sun as we watched the helicopter descend toward a large white boat some ways out on the water. As we watched, it landed, like a bee alighting on a flower. A few minutes later, we saw the boat turn toward the inn.

"That is a massive yacht," I said. "If he's got that, why is he staying with us?"

"He doesn't like sleeping on it," John said. "He gets seasick."

"I guess that's good news for us," I said.

∽

BY THE TIME the yacht slowed to a halt a ways from the inn and a small powerboat with Brandon and his entourage launched itself toward the inn, I'd spruced myself up a bit and John had done a last check of the upstairs room.

"Everything ship-shape?" I asked.

"I certainly hope so," he said. As we watched, a young woman I was guessing must be a deckhand nimbly tied the boat up to our dock. A moment later, a slight man in a heavy black jacket and dark blue skinny jeans alighted from the vessel, followed by a young man and a young woman, both also clad in black and laden with heavy bags.

"Here we go," I said, as we walked out to welcome Brandon Marks, prodigy and multimillionaire several times over.

"Welcome to the Gray Whale Inn," I said in a cheery voice as he mounted the back steps to the porch, his attendants in his wake.

To my surprise, the young woman, who was carrying a duffel bag almost as big as she was herself, smiled and responded. "Thank you so much. I'm Brandon's assistant, Rebecca Vick, and this is my associate, Antoine Sperry." She had unbelted her black trench coat; beneath it, she was neatly dressed in gray slacks, modest flats, and a silk blouse, her shoulder-length hair cut on an angle sloping toward her chin. Antoine, on the other hand, looked like a club bouncer; his black T-shirt stretched over disturbingly large biceps, and he wore black jeans and black sneakers to match. A tattoo that appeared to involve bones and possibly two skulls wound up his left arm. I presumed he was something of a bodyguard, and I wondered why Brandon felt he needed one. "We'll be escorting Mr. Marks to his room," Rebecca announced. "Do you have the key?" As she spoke, Brandon, appearing completely disinterested in the proceedings, stared out toward the water.

"Where is the site?" he asked, as if nobody else had spoken.

"It's a mile or two out. I'll be happy to take you there in my skiff if you'd like," John offered.

Brandon didn't answer, but continued to gaze out at the water. I was irked at his rudeness; we were not off to a smashing start.

"Follow me and we'll get you all checked in," I said. John relieved Rebecca of the heavy duffel bag as I led them inside, then through the swinging door that led to the rest of the inn from the kitchen. Brandon followed, ensconcing himself in one of my overstuffed parlor chairs as Antoine lugged the rest of the bags in and I worked with Rebecca to distribute room keys.

"We'll help you with the luggage," I offered.

"Wonderful," she said. "You've got everything on the checklist taken care of? Detergent, food requirements, the rest of the upstairs blocked off?"

"Of course," I said, hoping Catherine arrived before Brandon requested coffee with coconut oil, stevia, and collagen powder in it. I was handing Rebecca the three keys when voices sounded from the downstairs hallway; a moment later, Max and Ellie appeared.

"Hi, ladies!" I said, smiling at them.

"Hey!" Max replied with a slight smile. Max was an attractive woman who, she had told me, had twin girls about to start college; combined with her very recent divorce, she was facing a lot of big changes, fast. She'd looked like she hadn't slept for a week when she arrived, but now, there were roses in her cheeks and a bit of a sparkle in her brown eyes.

"Whatever you're doing seems to be working," I informed her companion, Ellie, who ran a bookstore in Boston. "She looks much better."

"I keep telling her she'll be in fighting shape in no time," Ellie replied with an infectious smile.

"The rest of the keys?" Rebecca said with a note of irritation that told me she was used to being top priority.

"Here they are," I said, handing them to her. "Have fun, ladies!" I called as Max and Ellie let themselves out the front door.

"We will," Ellie said. "And don't worry about dinner for us; we'll be at Spurrell's."

"Got it," I told them, adding "Don't miss the clam chowder!" before they closed the front door behind them.

"Thanks for your patience," I said as I returned my attention to Rebecca, who was now drumming her fingers on the top of the desk. "Do you still want to use the same credit card?"

"Yes," she said shortly. "And as I'm sure you're aware, Mr. Marks will be needing his afternoon juice in..." she checked her watch "... twenty-three minutes. You can deliver it to my room, and I'll take it to him."

"Sure," I said, glancing at John, who was watching the proceedings with barely concealed amusement.

"I'll take care of it," he volunteered, and headed to the kitchen while I finished checking them in.

"You remember we'll be needing an early breakfast in the morning?" she asked.

"Of course," I said. "We'll have it ready at seven."

"I understand your husband has some interest in military history," she said.

"Yes," I confirmed. "He's really excited about the discovery."

"Mr. Marks has offered to allow you to accompany him to the research vessel to watch the submersible video the wreck," she said, the twist of her mouth suggesting she thought it was a dreadful idea.

"Really?" I asked. The big man himself apparently didn't speak for himself; it was a bit odd, but I couldn't complain. "John will be thrilled... thank you so much!"

"Thank Mr. Marks," she said, pocketing the keys. I glanced over at Brandon Marks, wondering if he would respond, but he just sat motionless, gazing out the window. Friendly guy. "Anything else?" Rebecca asked in that efficient tone of voice.

"No," I said. "I'll take that duffel up," I told her, "and if you'd like to leave the rest of the bags down here, John and I can take them."

"I'll take them myself," Antoine answered in a surprisingly low voice. They were the first words I'd heard him say. He appeared to be in his early thirties, with a handsome face and his features set in a pleasant expression, but I got the impression of something dangerous lurking beneath the calm exterior. I was guessing Antoine did more for Brandon than just lug his bags.

"If you change your mind, let me know," I said. "Your rooms are at the end of the upstairs hall. We'll have that juice up shortly. Would you two like anything?"

"No thank you," Antoine said, glancing at Brandon as if

to warn him off asking for anything. Although I doubted the odds of that were very high, based on our interaction to date.

"We'll just head up now," Rebecca said. "Thank you," she added in a dismissive tone.

"You're welcome," I told her, but she had already turned away and was heading up the stairs while Brandon stood silent in the front hall.

"Aren't you guys going up, too?" I asked Antoine.

He shook his head. "Not until she's checked everything out."

"Got it," I said. "When do you head out to see the submersible, by the way?"

"Eight a.m.," he said.

Right at breakfast. I wasn't sure Gwen would be able to handle things, but I was hoping Catherine might want to pitch in; I didn't want to miss the chance to be the first to see a U-Boat that had been hidden deep in the ocean since the end of World War II. "Thanks," I told him. He gave me a slight nod in response. Brandon, on the other hand, was still staring out the window. Was he incapable of speech?

"We'll be there," I said. "Thanks for the opportunity."

"Again, thank Mr. Marks," he said.

I did as he suggested, calling out a cheery "Thank you so much for the opportunity."

"You're welcome," Brandon said in a rote voice, still staring out the window.

"Please let me know if there's anything you need while you're here," I said.

A moment later, Rebecca came trotting downstairs and gathered up Brandon like a mother duck retrieving a lost duckling. "It's all good. Follow me please, Mr. Marks," she said in an brisk yet deferential tone.

He did as she bade him, following her up the stairs, Antoine behind him. I watched them go. What an odd trio, I thought to myself.

And what a strange, solitary life Brandon Marks seemed to lead.

~

CHARLENE WAS PACING BACK and forth behind the counter when I got to the Cranberry Island General Store and Post Office. I'd left John in charge of the inn, and promised to tell him as soon as I knew more about Tania; now, as I stepped into the familiar little store, I hoped I could do something to help my friend, who was both postmistress and storekeeper, and had created this cozy space.

The squishy couch and chairs in the front, which was known as the island's living room, beckoned invitingly, and the smell of coffee filled the store. All kinds of necessities, from motor oil to trout pâté from the mainland, lined the small store's shelves, and a cake stand with a few pieces of one of my blueberry coffee cakes stood next to the register —I tried to keep Charlene supplied with sweets for her customers. A wall of mailboxes stood behind the counter; since everyone on the island had to come to the store to pick up mail or send anything off, Charlene saw everyone who lived here, and had her finger on the pulse of the island. If she didn't know where Tania was, I thought with an uncomfortable twist in my stomach, then odds were good she wasn't on the island.

"No word?" I asked; unnecessarily, since Charlene's normally flawless hair was hanging around her face, and she hadn't even bothered with mascara. She was definitely not her normal self.

"Nothing," she said. "I call her every two minutes, and no answer. Her friend Megan isn't answering her phone, either." She ran a hand through her hair. "I want to go over there and pound on her door... and Megan's, too."

"Do it," I said. "I'll watch the store."

"Are you sure?"

"Positive," I said. "John said he'll call the mainland police if she's not there."

"Thank you," she said, and grabbed a jacket off the hook by the door, practically sprinting to the front of the store.

As I fretted about Tania and waited for Charlene to return, I poured myself a cup of coffee and picked up the copy of the *Daily Mail* that sat on the counter. At the bottom of the front page was an article on the U-Boat discovery, and the mysterious man who had funded the team that located it.

"Little is known about Mr. Marks's personal life," I read. "He lives in San Francisco, California, and does not give media interviews. He is, however, known for his fascination with military history, and has funded the Blue Diver research vessel for the last three years as it has scoured the floor of the Atlantic looking for wrecks."

Nothing I didn't already know, although I did wonder why he was so interested in military history.

"The vessel located by Marks's team is thought to be the U-Boat 809, a U-Boat that prowled the Maine coast during World War II and is thought to be responsible for the sinking of at least nine boats, including several vessels local to the area."

I hadn't thought about the terror fishermen and sailors must have felt. Although no foreign power had invaded US soil, the water was a different thing entirely, and most folks in this part of the world had family or friends who spent a good part of their time at sea.

"The reclusive millionaire is staying on Cranberry Island during his stay; the island is thought to have suffered many casualties as a result of the U-Boat," the article went on.

No wonder there was so much interest on the island, I realized. The sunken submarine had likely been responsible for the loss of the ancestors of several of my neighbors. Including Murray Selfridge, the real estate developer who had built one of the ugliest houses on the island (in my opinion, anyway) and who until recently had been dating my mother-in-law.

As I reread the article, Eleazer Spurrell walked into the store. I was very fond of Eli, who was a cheerful, thoughtful man with bright eyes that missed absolutely nothing. He had been the island's boatwright for as long as anyone could remember, and had built both my skiff and John's. His wife, Claudette, was the owner of two goats, Muffin and Pudge, who, although very cute and lovable, were the bane of the gardens on the island. When the door closed behind him, Eli paused and blinked at the sight of me behind the counter.

"Second job?" he asked.

"No," I said. "I'm filling in for Charlene; Tania's gone missing, and she's going to see if she might be at Megan's place. Have you seen her at all the last day or two?" I asked.

"Afraid not," he said. "Maybe she went over to the mainland?"

"She wouldn't do that without telling Charlene," I said. "She's always been responsible."

"I'll keep an ear to the ground," he said.

"If she's not at Megan's place, I'm going to ask John to get in touch with the mainland and file a missing persons report," I told him.

"I hope it doesn't come to that," he said, eyeing the goodies on the cake plate. "One of those, please, and a cup of coffee."

"Of course," I said, putting a slice of blueberry coffee cake on a plate and setting it in front of him, then filling a mug. Claudette had Eli on a strict sugar-free diet, despite the fact that he was one of the wiriest men I knew, so I'd secretly been supplying him with baked goods for years. "Mail, too?"

"If you don't mind," he said. As he bit into the piece of cake, I retrieved the key to his mailbox, unlocked the little cubby, and pulled out a sheaf of envelopes, setting them next to his plate.

"Thank you kindly," he mumbled through a mouthful of crumbs. "That millionaire's over at your place now, isn't he?"

"He flew in by helicopter this morning," I confirmed.

"More money than sense," he said. "Although I'm mighty glad he found the U-boat. That nasty thing probably sank my grandfather's ship; he was a merchant marine at the time."

"I had no idea," I said. "I'm so sorry."

"It was a long time ago," he said. "I never got to meet him, but my grandmother was never the same after she lost him. He had about six other local boys working for him; it hit the island hard."

"That's horrible," I said. "Why does everyone think this missing submarine was responsible?" I asked.

"Everyone knew there was a U-Boat out there preying on ships. Some of them used to use the lights of towns on the coast to locate boats; there was such fear back then, boats used to move in convoys, like schools of fish, for protection. For months, boats were sinking left and right... and then, all of a sudden, it stopped."

"So they think it was because the U-Boat responsible sank?"

"We were still in the middle of the war, so you can bet nobody was callin' off the dogs, so to speak. Something must have happened to it to make it stop, at least that was the idea."

"How will we know if this was the submarine that did it?"

"A few of the ships have been investigated over the years, and torpedo damage was confirmed. Even if it weren't, some of the vessels went down in sight of land, so there were witnesses. A few survivors said they went down because they were torpedoed, and the wrecks bear that out. If there is a U-Boat off the coast, odds are good it was the source of it."

"That must be a horrible way to go," I said. "Sinking in a metal can."

"They sank a lot of ships before they went down," Eli pointed out. "They only got what they dished out." I could sense the wound was still not entirely healed.

"Well, we'll find out soon enough. They're going down with a submersible tomorrow morning to film the wreck. Brandon invited John and me to go out with them."

"Tell me what you see, will you?" he asked. "Everybody always wondered why the attacks suddenly stopped. It would be good to put that chapter to rest."

"I will," I said as he sipped his coffee. I turned to tidy up some of the mail boat schedules next to the register when Charlene burst into the store.

"She's not there," she said, eyes wild. "She's not

answering phone or text, she hasn't been on social media, and I ran into Theo Fleming, the guy she was seeing a while back, and he said he hasn't seen her in a while. Something's happened to her; I just know it."

My stomach twisted, and I caught Eli's eye; he looked as grim as I felt. "I'll call John now."

3

"I'll call the mainland right away," John promised when I told him what Charlene had reported. "Who are her closest friends on the island?"

"She hangs out with Megan a lot," I said, looking at Charlene. "Was Megan home?"

"Nobody answered the door, and Megan still isn't answering my calls."

I shared what Charlene had said with John.

"When was she last seen?" he asked.

"You last saw her yesterday, right?" I asked Charlene.

She nodded. "She took the morning shift and left at noon."

"Did Tania say anything about where she was going when she left the store?"

"Home for lunch. That's it."

"Anything weird?"

"She's been acting distracted lately, but I know she was struggling with one of her online math classes, so I figured that was it."

"Did she have a study buddy?"

"Actually, yes," Charlene said. "But she didn't say anything about meeting up when she left."

"Who is it?"

"Someone named Hunter," she said.

"Unusual name, at least. Let's call the school and see if we can find out more about this Hunter person."

"Good call," she said, sounding relieved.

I turned my attention to John, who had been listening to my end of the conversation, and relayed what Charlene had told me about her study buddy.

"I'll get on it; they should be able to release that information to me," he said. I put Charlene on the phone; she gave John details of the school Tania was attending online, and the name of the class, and hung up looking slightly better.

At least I thought so, until she said, "I hope this Hunter guy's not an axe murderer. Who names a kid Hunter, anyway?"

"A good swath of parents twenty years ago, in my experience," I told her, and put my hand on hers. "I'm sure we'll find her," I said with forced cheer.

~

THE ABSENCE of Tania weighed heavily on me the rest of the day, as it did on John. Gwen came down before dinner, looking revived and fresh in jeans, boots, and a black cowl-neck sweater that set off her pale skin and dark hair. For such a small island, Gwen, Charlene, and Catherine sure kept the fashion bar high, I thought. And then there was me, who favored loose jeans, flannel, and big wool sweaters most of the time. Thankfully, John didn't seem to mind.

"How are you feeling?" I asked.

"Better. Everything okay?" she asked, sensing the mood in the kitchen.

"Tania's gone missing," I said.

"What?"

"She told Charlene she'd be gone for a bit, and now she's not answering her phone and isn't at home."

"Maybe she's staying with a friend on the mainland?" Gwen suggested. "Cell service can be spotty sometimes, depending on where you are."

"I hope so," I said.

"Are you okay if I don't help with dinner?" she asked. "I don't want to push it."

"No problem," I said as she headed upstairs. "Let me know if you need anything."

"Thanks," she said, ducking her head down to give me a smile.

∼

Although dinner was small, preparing it was stressful. How often do you cook for someone who doubtless dines in the finest restaurants worldwide?

"It's a terrific dish," John reassured me as he mixed the sauce for the bok choy about a half hour before dinner. "You've made it dozens of times before, and it's always a hit."

"But most of my customers aren't reclusive gazillionaires."

"Stop worrying so much," he said as he tasted the sauce and added a touch of sesame oil. "It'll be fine."

I looked up at him. "Do you think Tania will be fine?"

"The college gave me Hunter's information. I left a message for him, and the mainland police are running his information for me. I'm going to swing by and talk with Charlene more tonight, see if there's anything she left out."

"Why don't we invite her over to the inn?" I suggested. "I'm sure she could use the company."

"Good idea," he said.

"I hope Tania's okay."

"Me too," he said as he sliced the end off a baby bok choy. Despite the coziness of the kitchen, with its white-curtained windows, warm yellow walls, and old pine farm table, it felt as if a dark cloud had descended over the inn. We worked in silence, both lost in thought.

Dinner was a small affair, consisting of Brandon and his two assistants, who ate without talking, which was odd considering they'd come all this way to see a wreck that had been lost since World War II.

"I didn't realize there were U-Boats so close to the Maine coast," I said once I'd placed their plates in front of the trio—soy-glazed, rare salmon, rice and stir-fried bok choy in a delicate sesame sauce

"Oh, they were all up and down the coast," Rebecca replied. "Mr. Marks told me that one of them actually dropped a pair of spies off in Bar Harbor."

"You're kidding me. That's only a few miles away from here!"

"I know; weird to think about, isn't it?" she said. For the first time, Brandon seemed to have noticed my existence. He studied me with dark eyes in a way that made me slightly uncomfortable, although I couldn't have said why. For just a moment, I could sense the intensity that had catapulted him to the top of his field; then, as if he'd flipped a switch, it was gone, and he was gazing out the window again, his expression blank. "They sure did a lot of damage," Rebecca went on as I watched Brandon.

"So I'm learning," I said. "What sparked your fascination with U-Boats?" I asked Brandon directly.

Rebecca jumped in to answer, but Brandon held up a narrow hand and turned to focus on me again. Less laser-like, but still intense.

"I wasn't looking for a U-Boat in particular," he said slowly, "but it is an intriguing find. And I do have a personal interest of sorts."

"Really? What's that?" I asked.

"I lost my great-grandfather to a U-Boat on the Grand Banks," he said calmly. "His name was Hezekiah Spurrell. He was the master of a merchant vessel; when the ship was hit, he refused to board a lifeboat and went back to save as many of his crew as he could." He shook his head. "He was last seen on the deck with a lantern before it went down."

"Master is like a captain, right?"

"Correct," he said.

"Wow," I breathed. "He was a good leader."

"He was," Brandon agreed with a sharp nod. I wondered if that was where he'd gotten his abilities from, although something about Brandon told me he might not be last on board to look for survivors. Still, it was hard to tell about people. I'd learned that over the years, for sure.

"Interesting that his name was Spurrell," I said. "There are Spurrells on Cranberry Island; it's an unusual name."

"From England, originally. And yes; it is unusual."

"Are you related in some way?"

"I don't believe so," he said. "My mother's side of the family hailed from Newfoundland, not Maine."

"Those sailors got around," I said. "You might want to check in with the Spurrells down at the lobster pound and ask if they've got some family trees." Not that he'd necessarily want to be related, I reflected; there had been one or two bad eggs in recent generations.

"No," he said peremptorily. "My family is not from here."

"Well," I said, sensing a sudden chill and wondering what had caused it. Brandon certainly was mercurial. "I should let you eat. Thank you for telling me about your family's history; I'm sorry it was such a dark chapter for your great-grandfather."

"He died a hero," he said. "That's more than most of us can say."

He wasn't wrong, I reflected as I retreated to the kitchen.

∽

THE TRIO WENT upstairs just after dinner, and as I cleared the dining room, Charlene knocked at the door. I opened it; I could tell by the empty look in her eyes that there was still no sign of Tania.

"Still no word," she said bleakly. "I'm just a mess."

"Come have some coffee cake," I said, giving her a big hug and leading her over to the kitchen table. "I'll put the kettle on for tea."

"Thanks," she said weakly. I settled her in, filled the kettle and took the foil off the coffee cake, cutting her a big piece of the moist, apple-studded cake. Then I hesitated and cut two more for John and me. After all, I only had two gluten-tolerant guests to feed in the morning.

As I set plates in front of John and Charlene and then sat down across from them, Catherine breezed into the kitchen, cheeks pink from the chill autumn breeze that had kicked up when the sun went down. "That was fun! I love being on the water in fall weather."

"Good dinner with your friend?" I asked.

"It was," she said. "And I got the coconut oil." She pulled the jar out of her pocket and set it on the counter. "Zelda was delightful; do you know she just got back from a month in Paris? Sometimes I think I should swear off men altogether and just live with women." She glanced at her son. "No offense, of course."

"None taken," he said drily, and we exchanged glances. Catherine had broken up with her steady, Murray Selfridge, not long ago, and although she hadn't exactly been mopey, she was still recovering. "Is the kettle on?" she asked as she unbelted her jacket.

"It is; you're welcome to some. I've got apple coffee cake, too."

"I'll pass on the cake, but tea would be great." She hung up her jacket and joined us at the kitchen table. As she sat, she noticed Charlene's wan face and John's dour look. "Oh, no. What happened? Did the millionaire not show up, or something?"

"Brandon Marks is here," I said. "But Tania's missing."

"Tania? Missing?" A delicate crease appeared between Catherine's arched brows. She and her son shared few features—she was delicate and refined, whereas John had a rugged handsomeness that always made me think he belonged on the front cover of an LL Bean catalogue—but they were both extraordinarily good-looking people. And good people, too, which was even more important. "I just saw her last night!"

We all sat up straighter. "What? Where?" Charlene asked.

"On the mail boat. She was headed over to the mainland. She had a small bag with her and her nose in a book, so I didn't disturb her, but I just figured she was going to do errands, or go to the library."

"Did anyone meet her at the dock?"

Catherine shook her head. "If they did, I didn't notice, I'm afraid. But surely she'll be back soon." At the lack of response from Charlene, she added, "Don't you think?"

"She's not answering her phone," Charlene said. "No texts, no social media... it's like she's vanished."

"Maybe her phone died," I suggested. "On the plus side, at least Catherine saw her this morning; maybe she'll be back late tonight."

"I came in on the last mail boat," Catherine said.

"Was she on the boat?" I asked.

Catherine shook her head. "No, but she could have come back earlier."

"She wasn't at home when I went," Charlene said.

"Does Tania have a land line?" I asked Charlene.

"No," she answered.

The kettle started to whistle; I got up and turned off the burner, then filled the tea pot. "Well, let's get that tea to go and we'll go check out her place," I suggested.

"I've already been over there, but it couldn't hurt to go again. I've got a spare key in my purse," Charlene said. "Let's go now, and if she's there, we can bring her back and all share."

Fair enough. "I'll drive," I offered, and Charlene and I hurried out of the inn together, both grabbing our jackets but not taking the time to put them on.

"Call as soon as you know anything," John said.

"Of course," I assured him.

~

IT WAS ONLY about a five-minute drive to Tania's little one-room cottage, like to anywhere else on the island, so it wasn't a particularly long trip, but it sure felt that way to both of us. I resisted the urge to speed down the lanes; there were too many cyclists and pedestrians on the island to risk it.

"Down here," Charlene said, directing me down a wooded dirt track to the left of the road. I turned the van onto it, hoping we'd see lights burning in Tania's cottage through the leaves, but the little building at the end of the track was dark.

"Damn," Charlene said under her breath. I parked the van in the empty spot outside the cottage and hurried after Charlene, who was already pounding on the door by the time I closed the van door behind me.

When no one answered, she fumbled with the key and threw open the door.

"Tania!"

She wasn't there. Charlene flicked on the light to reveal a cozy, tidy space.

The cottage was actually more like a cabin, with wood walls and exposed rafters. Red gingham curtains framed the windows, and Tania's neatly made bed was tucked in the far corner, with a bright white duvet with red and red-and-white checked pillows. A gray couch with a red throw pillow sat in the other corner, along with a small coffee table that looked vintage; a few *House Beautiful* magazines were interspersed with *Us!* and *Cosmos* on the white-painted top.

The kitchen was small, but functional, with a white tile counter, a two-burner stove, and an under-the-counter fridge. It was a lovely little set-up; the only thing missing was the lovely young woman who lived here.

"Where could she be?" Charlene mused as we stood in the vacant cottage. As she spoke, there was an insistent meow from behind the small kitchen table, and an orange-

and-white cat stood up, stretched, and padded over to greet us.

"Butters!" Charlene said, reaching down to scoop up the kitty, whose purring was so loud it was practically vibrating the house. "Where's your mom?"

Butters didn't answer, of course; instead he just burrowed his head under Charlene's chin.

"Should I take him home with me for now?" she asked.

"If it would make you feel better, then do it," I suggested. "He's still got food and water; she didn't leave him high and dry."

"Of course she didn't," Charlene sniffed.

"If you think it's best to take him, just leave a note for Tania, so she doesn't panic when she gets home."

"*If* she gets home," Charlene corrected me.

"Catherine saw her this morning. Maybe she just got held up and is going to take a water taxi over." Although I was also worried about Tania, I could sense that Charlene needed reassurance.

"She never does that. Too expensive."

"Maybe this time will be an exception," I said, but it was obvious Charlene wanted none of it. "In the meantime," I said, changing tack, "let's look around and see if there's any indication of where she might have gone. I don't see a purse or keys or anything, so there's that."

"True," Charlene said. "Sorry, Butters. Auntie Charlene has to do some investigating. You can come home with me in a bit."

Butters protested as she put him down, but a moment later he strolled over to me, looking up at me with winsome golden eyes.

"I'll give you a few pets, but I have to help your auntie," I informed him.

Tania was evidently a bit of a neatnik, so there wasn't much to root through in her cottage. A mail sorter at the end of the counter contained two utility bills and a credit card bill, which Charlene scanned, looking for anomalies. "I feel a little weird looking through these, honestly."

"I get it. It's up to you," I said.

She closed her eyes and thought about it for a moment, then opened them. "I don't like doing it, but my gut tells me there's something wrong, so I'm going to. I'll apologize later."

"That makes sense," I said as she opened an envelope.

"Well, she sure does eat at the Little Notch Bakery a lot," she said as she scanned the bill.

"In Northeast Harbor? I didn't know she went over there that often."

"I didn't either," she said. "Maybe her study buddy works there?"

"Or maybe that's where they meet," I suggested. "It's worth checking out, anyway."

"She's also got a charge here for some kind of testing place," Charlene said.

"What's that?"

"I don't know, but it shows up twice—once two weeks ago, and once two weeks before that."

"Write it down," I said. "Anything else?"

"Not really," she said. "She's not a big spender."

As Charlene looked through the bills, I walked around Tania's small space, looking for anything with a name on it or anything that looked out of place. In the bathroom, I found a surprise.

"Hey," I said. "There's a second toothbrush in here. And Old Spice deodorant."

"What?" Charlene asked, abandoning the mail sorter and joining me in the bathroom. "Whose is that?"

"I don't know. Is she seeing anyone?"

"If so, she hasn't told me about it," Charlene said. Then her eyes got big. "Do you think maybe she went out on a date and took up with a serial killer? Maybe he lured her to the mainland and killed her?"

"Odds are low," I pointed out. She really was struggling if she was leaping to such outlandish conclusions.

"Yes... but why didn't she tell me if she was seeing someone?"

"We don't know that she is," I reminded her. "And if she is, maybe it's early days. Maybe she's not sure what she thinks of him. Or maybe she's not sure you'll approve?'

"Well, I certainly don't now," my friend said. "I can't believe she didn't tell me, though. Why not?"

I had a few ideas, but decided it was best not to float them. "Maybe when we get in touch with Hunter he'll be able to shed some light on the situation. Any other people she hung out with on the island?"

"Mainly Megan," she said. "I'll bet she knows about whoever owns that Old Spice."

"You know where she lives, right? You were there earlier."

"You bet your bippy I do, and yes, I was there earlier," she said. "And we're going to talk to her right now."

"Are we taking Butters, or not?" I asked.

She looked over at the big orange cat, who was sprawled out on Tania's bed and appeared very relaxed. "I'll leave him here for now," she said. "I'll check on him tomorrow, if Tania's not back by then."

"That works for me," I said, and turned out the light as we headed out of the little cottage. Despite my encouraging words, my instincts were buzzing; there was something very not right about the situation.

I just hoped it didn't mean Tania was in serious trouble.

4

Megan still lived with her parents, and it was her mother, June, who answered the door, wearing a towel turban and a pink and blue housedress that made her look as if she'd just teleported in from the 1950s. A white Schnauzer was at her feet, barking and eyeing us with a mix of interest and suspicion.

"Charlene! Natalie! Is everything okay?" she asked.

"We're looking for Tania," Charlene informed her. "Is Megan home?"

"She just finished painting her toenails; come on in," June said. "Relax, Duchess," she admonished the little white dog, holding her by the collar as we stepped into the small front hall.

"Feel free to sit down," she said, gesturing to a small living area that hailed from the same era as her housedress. "I'll go find her."

Charlene and I perched on the edge of a long pink couch that had been brand-new and doubtless modern in the mid-twentieth century, but had obviously seen a good bit of wear over the years. Once we made it into the living room, Duchess seemed to decide we were okay, since she hurled herself up between us on her short stubby legs and threw herself across my lap, staring up at me with big brown eyes. I scratched behind her ears and she made a grunting noise, leaning into my hand with obvious pleasure, as I looked around.

Everything in the Canfields' living room looked as if it had remained unchanged for decades, from the Hummel figurines on the hutch along the paneled wall to the ancient tube television with rabbit ears, complete with tinfoil, in the corner of the room. Despite its vintage origin, everything was neatly kept; there was a tidy stack of Daily Mails next to the fireplace, the green carpet showed recent vacuum lines, and there was not a speck of dust anywhere. Whoever was in charge of the house—likely June—was a good housekeeper, and took care of her possessions. I was guessing the house had been in the family for several decades, with very little change.

"Did anyone in your family collect Hummel figurines?" Charlene asked as we waited, staring at the lines of shepherdesses on the shelves against the wall.

"My grandmother in Pennsylvania," I said. "I have no idea what happened to them, but she cherished them."

"My grandmother did, too," she said. As she spoke, there was a thump in the hallway, and June's mother, Edna, appeared, her gnarled hands gripping the handles of a walker.

"We don't usually have company at this time of day," she said with a smile, her blue eyes bright. "What brings you two here?"

"We're looking for Charlene's niece Tania," I informed her.

"Disappeared?"

"We're hoping she just got stranded on the mainland or something," I said. "We thought maybe Megan might know."

"Hmmm," she said. "They get into trouble at that age, don't they? Follow their hearts instead of their heads."

Something about the way she said it made my ears perk up. "Do you know anything about who Tania might be involved with?"

"I overheard her and Megan talking the other day. They think I can't hear, but when I turn these things up just right, I can hear a mosquito land a half mile away."

"What were they talking about?"

Edna glanced over her shoulder and shuffled forward a few steps before telling us. "Tania got herself mixed up with someone she shouldn't have. Megan was telling her it wasn't worth it, but you know how young girls are."

My heart squeezed with foreboding. "What do you mean, 'someone she shouldn't have'?"

She glanced over her shoulder again. "I don't know, but Megan said that nothing good would come of it. And she's got a good head on her shoulders." Edna tapped her head. "Comes from my side of the family."

As she spoke, I caught a whiff of acetone. Megan had arrived. She was cozied up in flannel pajamas covered in white rabbits and was holding her hands out in front of her, the purple nail polish fresh and shiny. Her mother was a few steps behind her.

"Hey," she said, giving her grandmother a careful side hug so as not to mess up her nails.

"Can I get you all a cup of tea or something?" June asked.

"No, thanks... we're good," Charlene said.

"What's up?" Megan asked, sitting down on the baby-blue love seat across from us.

"We're still looking for Tania," I told her.

Her eyes grew wary... and, unless I was mistaken, a little bit afraid. "She's not back yet?"

"No," I said. "We were wondering if you had any idea who she might be with, or where she might have gone."

"Is she seeing that Hunter guy?" Charlene blurted out.

"Hunter?" Megan looked confused for a moment. "Oh, Hunter. Her friend from online school. No... he's got a boyfriend," she said.

"She's seeing someone, though," Charlene said.

Megan blinked her big brown eyes, trying to look as if she didn't know what Charlene was talking about. "How do you know?"

"I didn't just fall off the turnip truck," Charlene said. "I know she asked you to keep it under your hat, but she's missing, and we need to know who she's seeing. She could be in trouble."

Megan glanced at her mother, and then her grandmother, who gave her a short, decisive nod. "Whatever you know, tell them," she said. "If your friend's in a pickle, she'll need all the help she can get."

Megan's shoulders sagged. "She made me swear not to tell anyone."

Charlene and I waited for her to continue.

"Go on, girl," her grandmother prompted.

"I don't know his last name," Megan said, twisting a strand of hair and not meeting our eyes, "but she's been hanging out with this guy in his mid-thirties, and his name is Dan."

"Where does he live?" Charlene asked, rapid-fire.

"Somewhere on Mount Desert Island," she answered. "She told me he has a house, but I don't know where it is."

"Dan on Mount Desert Island," Charlene said. "That certainly narrows it down."

"I'm sorry," Megan said, voice rising. "That's all she told me."

"But you didn't think it was a good idea, did you?" I asked in a gentle tone.

"How do you know that?" Megan asked, her eyes briefly darting to mine, and then away.

"I told her," her grandmother confessed.

"You heard us?"

"I hear more than you know, my dear. Just because I'm old doesn't mean I'm deaf. Well, maybe I am deaf, but with these hearing aids I'm not."

"Why didn't you think it was a good idea?" I asked.

"He's just so much older. And they only meet in secret," she said.

"Why?"

"She wouldn't say. She just said... it's complicated." Again, her eyes were focused on her hair; she wasn't telling us everything she knew. I wasn't the only one who figured that out.

"I'll bet," said her grandmother dryly. "Married men always do say things like that."

Megan dropped the strand she was twisting and looked at her grandmother in horror. "Nan!"

"It's the oldest story in the book. I almost fell for it once myself."

"You?" Megan asked, as if the concept of her grandmother having anything even remotely approaching a romantic entanglement was about as likely as a jellyfish driving a car.

"Yes, me. I wasn't always this old, you know."

"I know... it's just..."

"It was before I met your grandfather, so don't worry. I

heard the same story, though, I'll bet. He's just waiting for the right time to leave, isn't he?" she asked.

"He was going to tell his wife he was leaving after Christmas," she admitted. "He even gave Tania a ring."

"Right," I said. "Was she going to visit him, do you know?"

She nodded. "His wife was out of town, so they were going to go on a trip together, just the two of them."

"Where?" Charlene almost barked, and I put a hand on her arm.

"I don't know!" Megan said in a frantic tone.

"So she scurried off to a bed and breakfast God knows where with a married man more than ten years her senior, and I didn't even know she was involved with him," Charlene said. "Terrific. Her mother's going to give me the Aunt of the Year award for sure."

"At least we know she didn't just vanish," I said.

"But we have no idea where she is," Charlene pointed out. "And she's usually very good about communicating things." There was fear in her eyes. I didn't blame her. We knew nothing about this man, except that he was a liar.

"I have a few friends who own B&Bs on the mainland," I said. "I'll ask around."

"How will you find her? She won't be using her name."

"I'll scan a picture," I said. "If they've got a young woman who looks like her staying, I'll send a picture to confirm."

"Good idea," she said. "And maybe John can get the police involved, too."

"But she's over 18!" Megan said. "She's not a kid anymore."

"She may be officially an adult," Charlene said, "But she's still a missing young woman... and my niece." She stared hard at Megan. "Anything else you remember? What kind of job he has, what he looks like, where they were going... anything at all?"

"No," she said miserably, this time meeting Charlene's eyes directly. "If I did, I'd tell you."

"Okay," my friend said. "You know where to reach me if you hear from her, though, right? Anytime, anywhere."

"I will," Megan promised.

"They usually come to their senses," Megan's grandmother reassured Charlene. "I did."

"I just hope it's not before something really bad happens," Charlene said.

So did I.

~

MAX AND ELLIE were in the parlor, drinking a bottle of white wine and munching on cookies, when we got back to the inn.

"What's wrong?" Max asked as we walked through the front door. She was sitting on a sofa with her legs tucked up beneath her, Ellie across from her.

"Can you tell?"

"You both look terribly worried," Max pointed out. "Do you need some wine? We're well-stocked."

"I think I'll take you up on that," Charlene said, plunking herself down on the couch. "My niece is missing," she added, then burst into tears.

"Oh, that's terrible," Max said, moving over to sit next to her on the couch. I touched my friend on the shoulder and said, "I'm going to go tell John what we learned so he can tell the folks on the mainland. I'll bring some glasses," I said. As Max comforted Charlene, I hurried into the kitchen to tell John what we'd learned.

"So at least we know she went to meet someone," he said. "It concerns me that she hasn't been in touch."

"Can we use the GPS on her phone to find her?" I suggested.

"I'm not sure we can without some kind of warrant," he said. "Besides, cell phone coverage is dicey in Maine."

"True," I agreed. "Max and Ellie have offered to share their wine; Charlene's out there now. I'm going to grab a few glasses and some cookies; do you want to join us?"

"Let me call the mainland and see what I can find out first," he said as I gathered glasses and tossed a bunch of oatmeal chocolate-chip cookies onto a plate. He was already on the phone by the time I pushed through the swinging door and hurried back to where Charlene was still sobbing quietly.

"How old is she?" Max was asking as I set the glasses and the cookies down on the table. Ellie filled two glasses, and I handed the first one to Charlene, who took a big swig before answering.

"Twenty going on about twelve, it seems. I'm embarrassed to tell you, but I think she got involved with someone she shouldn't have, and it kind of looks like they ran off together."

"Like, to get married?"

"I doubt that," Charlene said, "since he's already married."

"Ouch," Max said, wincing. "I wonder if his wife has any idea?"

"I don't know, since all I know about him is that his name is Dan and he lives on Mount Desert Island." She turned to me. "Did you tell John everything?"

"I did," I confirmed, sitting down on the other side of her. "He's on the phone with the mainland police now."

"Good," she said, and took another long swig.

"That's horrible, not knowing where she is, or who she's with. They can be so impetuous, can't they?"

"Totally," Charlene agreed.

"I can't imagine how I'd feel if it were one of my daughters," Max told her, compassion in her brown eyes. "They're only a few years younger, but they certainly have their own ideas about things. I'm sure she'll come to her senses and come back."

"I hope so," Charlene said. She sighed. "I wish Robert were here."

"You should call him," I suggested. "Maybe he'll be able to take a few days off and come up."

"He's in Australia for a week or two on business," she said with a sigh.

"Well, then, call him," I suggested. "I don't know what the time difference is, but at least text him and let him know what's going on. You need the support."

"You're right; I should do that. Will you excuse me for a minute?"

"Of course," I said, and she headed out to the back porch and dialed my cousin.

"You mentioned that you've got daughters," I said. "How are they doing?"

"No one's run off with anyone, to my knowledge anyway, but one of them isn't too happy with me right now," Max said with a rueful smile. "Her dad and I split up not long ago, and she's angry."

"That's hard," I said.

She shrugged. "Audrey seems fine with it—she says everything's less tense now—but Caroline is disappointed, disillusioned, and... well, I don't like to say the word, but she's pissed. At both of us, I think. And I don't know what to do about it."

"She'll be okay in the long run," Ellie reassured her. "You and Ted struggled for a long time to put things back together. You still both love them, and they know that. And I know you're better now."

"Do you?" Max said in a hollow voice. "Sometimes I feel better, but sometimes it just feels as if the world has been ripped out from under me."

"I'm so sorry," I said.

"Thanks," the dark-haired woman said, her eyes crinkling as she smiled at me. "And the kids aren't the only thing. I've got to move out of the house, and the Boston market is so expensive. I have no idea what to do for a place to live, or even work."

"I told you I'll promote you to assistant manager at the bookstore," Ellie suggested. "You're practically doing the job already."

"I'd love to, but long-term, I won't be able to afford to live in Boston. Besides," she said, twisting her long hair up into a knot on top of her head, "I think I'm ready for a fresh start. Too many ghosts in Boston."

"Have you thought about opening your own bookstore somewhere?" I asked.

She blinked at me. "No," she said, but she sounded intrigued. "How would I even go about doing that?"

"I had no innkeeping experience when I bought this place," I said, "so I learned on the job."

"How did you find it?"

"I came up here on vacation and fell in love with it," I said. "It was for sale, and there wasn't another inn on the island, so..." I shrugged.

"That was it?"

"That was it," I said. "And you've got more experience than I do. It sounds like you're already pretty familiar with the book business; it would be a lot easier for you."

"You mean... I should buy a bookstore?"

"Why not?" I asked, shrugging. "I've heard small bookstores are making a comeback. You could feature local books, have author signings, start a book group or writing group or two... I think it sounds like fun!"

"It is fun," Ellie confirmed.

"I... I've never thought about that before, but I kind of love that idea," she said. "But where?"

"Is there a place you love?" I asked.

"There is, actually," she said immediately. "Snug Harbor. I would have gone there, but I needed a break from my mother this week... she's still trying to come to terms with the break-up."

"Her mom's got a camp there, on Crescent Lake," Ellie explained. "I was thinking... I wonder if the current owner might be interested in giving up the store," she said.

Max sat up straight. "What? I practically grew up in that store! Loretta introduced me to Nancy Drew, Agatha Christie, *The Black Stallion*... why would she give it up?"

"She's not been in the best of health, from what I understand," Ellie said. "Maybe she'd be happy to let it go if she knew someone like you was going to take it over."

"Oh, no," Max said. "She just seemed so full of determination and energy I can't imagine her giving it up. But I haven't stopped into the store in a few years, what with everything going on in Boston, and last time it wasn't doing so well..." She turned her wine glass around in her hands. "I hate to think of anything happening to Loretta, or the store going away. But am I crazy to even think about talking to her about taking it over?"

"You're a natural," Ellie said. "And that could be just the thing. If she is ready to retire, I'm sure she'd be glad to know the store was in good hands."

"I'll think about it," Max said. "Of course, this could all be speculation..."

"I don't think so," Ellie told her. She pursed her lips, as if debating something, before continuing. "I didn't want to tell you until I knew for sure, but she's thinking it may be pancreatic cancer."

"Oh, no," Max breathed. "I have to go see her in any case, whether I end up doing anything with the store or not. Her guidance meant so much to me... without her, I might not have my love of books."

"I'm sure she'd appreciate knowing that," I said. "And who knows? You might be the new owner of the bookstore. What's it called, again?"

"Seaside Cottage Books," she said.

"Oh, yes. That sounds lovely."

"It is," Max said. "It's a little cottage right on the shore. Loretta used to have roses growing in the front, and a special room filled to the brim with kids' books and bean bags. I just can't believe she's sick."

As she spoke, Charlene walked back in, looking a little bit lighter. "What's going on?" she asked.

"We're trying to talk Max into buying a bookstore," Ellie said.

"A bookstore?"

"Now that my marriage is over, I need to find a way to support myself," Max said. "I've been out of the corporate job market since I got married, and I can't afford Boston, so they're encouraging me to look into a possible opportunity in the town I used to spend summers in as a kid."

"It's good to have a project after a break-up," Charlene

advised. "And a change of scenery doesn't hurt, either. I have more experience with that than I care to admit."

"Although you'd better not move," I warned her.

"Tell your cousin to behave and I won't have to!" she said with a slight grin.

"Is he coming down?"

"As soon as he's back from Australia," Charlene said. "We talk all the time, though."

"Good," Max said approvingly, refilling Charlene's glass as she spoke. "You need someone who will be there for you when the chips are down."

"To being there when the chips are down," Charlene said, raising her glass.

"And to Tania's speedy return," I added.

"And a full recovery for Loretta and a new project, in Snug Harbor or elsewhere, for Max," Ellie tossed in just before we clinked glasses.

∼

BY THE TIME the next morning rolled around, there was still no word from Tania, but John had mobilized the mainland police and they were combing through B&Bs up and down the coast. I'd fed Brandon and his entourage veggie omelets, bacon, and blueberry compote, and John and I were bundling up as Catherine went over the menu she'd be serving to Max and Ellie when they made it downstairs. Which could be a while; we'd stayed up rather late, and the two of them had polished off at least a bottle of wine between them.

"Still no word from the mainland police?" I asked John as we put on boots and heavy jackets for the trip out to the research vessel.

"None yet," he said. "I'm still hoping Tania just comes back on the mail boat."

"Me too," I said, grabbing a piece of apple coffee cake for the road, so to speak. "Want one?"

"Of course," he said, and I handed him a square in a napkin.

There was room for all of us on the boat Brandon had used to get to the island. As we walked down to join Brandon, Rebecca, and Antoine, I was surprised to see Eli near the stern of the boat.

"You're coming too?" I asked.

"Ayuh," he said. "When I reached out and told him about my grandfather, Mr. Marks was kind enough to let me come."

"Wonderful," I said, stepping aboard and sitting down near him. John hopped in after me; the young woman running the vessel untied the ropes and started the motor, and we were off.

"How far is it?" I asked Rebecca.

"Not too far," she said with a shrug, zipping up her down jacket and huddling into it, hands jammed into her pockets. Brandon's eyes were focused on the horizon, but he drummed his gloved fingers on the gunwale, in a rhythmic manner that probably would have annoyed me if I could hear it over the sound of the motor, the boat cutting through the waves, and the wind.

It was a chilly, gray morning, with a bit of wind on the water, making the ride somewhat choppy; I was glad I wasn't prone to seasickness. As the island receded, I dug a hat out of another pocket and pulled it down over my ears, wishing I'd thought to bring a scarf as well. As John reached for my hand, I glanced at him, smiling, and then looked back at the inn, a swell of gratitude and pride filling me.

The gray-shingled building nestled into the island as if it had always been there, tucked back into dark green pines and firs interspersed with the bright red and gold of deciduous trees. The blue window boxes held bright yellow mums and ivy, and the field below the inn, which in spring was a swathe of lupines, swept down to the rocky coast, the path to the dock lined with beach roses, the winey-scented blossoms of summer now replaced by golden-orange rose hips. The raspberry bushes by the tree line were turning from lime green to yellow, and I could spot the blueberry bushes dotting the cliffs next door by their brilliant rust-red color. Even the two apple trees I had planted a few years back next to the carriage house had turned a beautiful gold; I loved their blossoms in the spring, and the tart fruit they produced, but they were beautiful in any season.

The morning mail boat chugged by not far from us, heading for the Cranberry Island pier, and I squinted at it, hoping to see Tania, but everyone was under cover in the back, so it was impossible to tell. The lighthouse on the end of the island stood tall and proud, and I could make out the houses of some of the wealthier summer people, including the Jamesons, whose white mansion commanded a knoll with a sweeping view of the ocean. I'd only met Ed a few times since moving to the island; they had a gorgeous sailboat that he used to go back and forth from the mainland, and they kept to themselves, although occasionally I spotted a few children Charlene assured me were theirs tooling around the island. Since half the joy of living on Cranberry Island was the community, I didn't understand his reasoning, but some people like their privacy, I guess. Charlene told me he'd given a few lavish parties when she was young and the house had belonged to his parents, but those had faded, and he'd become something of a recluse, coming to the island less and less over the years.

"Look!" John said, pointing out an osprey wheeling overhead. As I looked up, it passed right over the boat, then winged toward the island, searching for breakfast in the waves below.

Before long, Cranberry Island shrank into the distance, and we were alone on the open water. Not for the first time, I was thankful for navigation equipment; with cloud cover and no landmarks in sight, it would be far too easy to be lost. I felt a wave of sympathy for the poor sailors who had gone down all those years ago... and for those they had taken down, including Eli's ancestor. Were we about to see the U-Boat that had terrorized Cranberry Island during World War II? Could it even be the submarine that had dropped two spies off on the mainland in the forties?

That was one of the things I loved about this part of the world: the history. It was everywhere, from the inn itself, to a secret compartment at the bottom of the lighthouse... we'd even discovered an old pirate ship deep under the waves a few years back.

And now, quite possibly, we were going to identify the remains of a vessel that hadn't been seen in 80 years.

Brandon continued drumming his fingers and staring out to sea while Antoine's eyes were trained on the GPS and the horizon. Rebecca was busy tapping away on her cell phone, and Eli, who was seated across from us, looked both excited and grim.

"How's Claudette?" I leaned in to ask Eli, talking loudly to be heard over the sound of wind and water.

"Better," he said. "The treatments seem to be working." Eli's wife Claudette had been diagnosed with Hodgkin's not long ago; I was glad to hear that she was improving. For a while, we'd been afraid it was something untreatable; although the treatments were an inconvenience, it was much better than the alternatives.

"I'm so glad," I told him. "And how about the grandkids?"

"They were just up over Labor Day weekend," he said. "Claudie even had enough energy to bake cookies with them."

"Cookies?" I asked, blinking. Claudette was known for her strict no-sugar stance.

"Chocolate chip," he said. "Full sugar. She's a sucker for her grandkids."

"Did you get a few?"

"She let me have two," he said. "That she knows of," he added with a wink.

I laughed and pulled my piece of apple cake out of my pocket. "You want this? I had a big breakfast; I don't think I can manage it."

"Are you sure?" he asked.

"I wouldn't offer if I wasn't," I said with a grin, watching as he took it eagerly; he always loved my baking, and it made me happy to see him smile.

He'd just finished off the last crumbs when a large research vessel came into view. Brandon sat up straighter, his eyes fixed on it, and even Rebecca stopped typing, instead holding up her phone to take a picture.

"There she is," Eli said as we approached the white vessel, which looked to be about a hundred feet long and was equipped with all kinds of antennae and satellite dishes. The young skipper slowed our boat and came around to the back of the research vessel. Eli jumped up and help him tie the ropes. Once we were secured, the young woman cut the engine and climbed the short ladder, then turned around held out a hand for Rebecca, who took it and gave her a grateful smile—the first real expression I'd seen. I followed, with John behind me, then Eli. Brandon and Antoine, to my surprise, were last off the boat.

We were greeted by a short woman wearing round glasses, her hair scraped back into a ponytail. She wore a bright orange jacket and rubber boots. "Good morning, Mr. Marks," she said. "It's good to see you again."

He shook her hand. "Everything ready?"

"We've got the submersible ready to go down," she said, pointing to a vehicle on the back of the boat that reminded me of the Mars Rover. "We'll have cameras so that those on the boat can watch. I'll be joining you on the way down."

He gave a short nod in response.

"If you'll come with me, we'll get you ready to go down. The rest of you can head inside with the crew," she directed us, indicating a young man in a heavy black jacket and red gloves. "There's coffee, and some breakfast if you're hungry."

"Thanks," I said, and we all followed him into the cabin, where a man and a woman were hunched over laptop computers.

"Hello!" said the woman, who was about my age and had curly red hair. "Come for the big reveal?"

"We did," Eli confirmed, looking at the laptop open in front of her. The screen was filled with a sonar image of the ocean floor. I could see what looked like a boat nestled into a valley on the sandy bottom.

"Is this it?" John asked quietly.

"That's what we're thinking," the woman said. "I'm Maureen, by the way. I'm one of the scientists working on this; Philip here is the captain." The man nodded, smiling.

We all introduced ourselves. When Eli spoke up, the captain looked at him. "You're the one who lost an ancestor to a U-Boat, then, right?"

"That's right," Eli confirmed, his eyes straying to the screen.

"How much will we be able to see?" John asked.

"The video should be fairly clear," Maureen said. "Depending on how cloudy the water is; there's a bit of chop, but it shouldn't affect the lower depths as much."

"How deep is she?" Eli asked.

"About 200 meters," she said. As she spoke, she glanced out the window. "They're about to go down. If you'll wait here, I'm just going to do one last check."

We waited in the cabin with the captain, watching through the window as Maureen hurried out to the deck and supervised Brandon and another crew member as they clambered into the submersible. A few minutes later, the big rover-looking vehicle was swung out over the side and began sinking into the dark water. Before long, it was out of sight.

"We're live," Maureen said as she hurried back into the cabin and turned on a big monitor near the front of the cabin.

The screen instantly filled with blackish green, little white spots swirling around. Something darted across the screen, flashing silver... a fish, most likely.

We watched, feeling a growing sense of anticipation, as the submersible continued to descend. Finally, after what felt like forever, the view seemed to bump a bit, and an image of the desolate sea floor emerged.

"All right," she said, then clicked on the radio she'd been holding. "You both okay down there?"

"Affirmative," came the answer.

"You've got the coordinates?"

"Affirmative," the radio crackled again.

"You're on the right track. Go slowly," she warned.

"Will do," the voice said. I glanced out at the dark water; it was hard to imagine that the murky scene on the screen was happening almost directly below us.

There wasn't much on the bottom of the sea. I spotted one crab scuttling into the distance, and the remains of an old-style wooden lobster trap which must have been lost decades ago; whatever had been inside it had long since escaped.

And then, as we watched, a gray, monolithic tube came into view, a small school of fish in front of it darting away from the beam of light.

"There it is," came the voice on the radio. I caught my breath.

"Is that really the U-Boat?"

"Looks like it," Eli said in a low voice as the beam traveled up the side to end abruptly.

"He's right," the red-haired scientist confirmed. "I don't know which one yet, but it's definitely not one of ours. And I'd say it was hit," she said as the beam focused on a metal plate that had been severed from the rest of the submarine. The tube looked as if it had been ripped into pieces by an angry child. I felt my chest tighten as I thought of the poor men inside.

"Torn to pieces," Eli said.

I tried to imagine what it would be like to have the explosion, and the lights going dark, and the water rushing in, but it was too much to consider. I focused on the screen as the beam moved away from the broken-up vessel and back into the empty sea bed.

The view returned to the sea floor. It had only gone a few yards when the submersible bumped into a strange-looking object on the floor of the ocean. Something shiny flashed in the light as the camera receded.

"Wait," Maureen ordered. "What's that?"

The submersible moved forward, training the light on the ocean floor. I could make out the shape of what looked like an anchor. Below it, as the beam moved, something flashed again.

"What is it?" I asked as the camera zoomed in.

"It looks like... a pendant?" John said, and then we all sucked in our breath.

Because the pendant lay on top of the collapsed remains of a ribcage.

5

"Could that be one of the submariners?" I asked, staring at the skeletal remains.

"Maybe," Eli said doubtfully, "but I don't know why it would be right under an antique anchor."

"Focus back in on the necklace, please," the scientist radioed the submersible. As it did, Eli let out a long sigh.

"What?" I asked.

"I think I recognize that necklace," he said. "And the person who wore it wasn't a sailor."

I looked at him. "Whose is it, then?"

He sighed. "A girl who disappeared a long, long time ago. Emmeline Hoyle's niece, Mandy."

John sucked in his breath.

"How can you tell?" I asked.

"She got that necklace from Emmeline on her confirmation day. Hope, Faith, and Charity," he said. He was right; I could make out the cross, the anchor, and the heart, all in gold.

"Oh, man," John breathed. "You're right."

"You knew her?"

"I hung out with her for a few summers; all the teenagers on the island did."

"That must have been scary when she disappeared."

"It was," he said. "At first we thought she ran off to the mainland, but when she didn't come back..." He shook his head.

"We still don't know for sure that it's her," I said. "There could be more than one necklace like that."

"There could be," Eli said, staring at the screens. "But what are the odds it would be right next to the killick that used to sit outside the museum?"

A chill swept through me as I stared at the screen. "A killick?"

Eli looked at me. "It's an old-style anchor with a piece of granite in a wooden frame. I'm a boatwright. And that's the same killick that sat outside the museum for more than twenty years. It went missing at the same time Mandy did."

John's face was set in a grim look. "We've got one disappeared young woman and we've discovered what we think might be another. It's not been a good couple of days."

"Who else is missing?" Eli asked.

"Tania," John said.

Eli shook his head. "I hope she comes to a better end than Mandy."

My stomach churned as the camera panned away from the golden necklace and John said, "I'm calling the mainland police."

∽

We'd started the morning with excitement, but the gruesome discovery had cast a pall over the proceedings. And there were still all the young German sailors that had been trapped in the U-Boat, too. I was glad when the submersible came back up; looking at the choppy, dark-blue water, studded here and there with lobster buoys, it was hard to imagine what was hidden far below.

The submersible popped open, and Brandon and the crewmember clambered out. As Brandon peeled off his wetsuit, he began talking for the first time. "We were the first ones to see it. After all these years. It's interesting that U-Boats usually go down in one piece."

"I didn't know that," Rebecca said, pushing a strand of hair out of her eyes. "Maureen is sending a copy of the video. Would you like to release it to the news outlets?"

"Yes, once you've finished the release. I'd like to let the German government notify the families first, though, once we've absolutely confirmed the U-Boat's identity," he said. "Do they really think that other body isn't part of the U-Boat crew?"

"It's not," Eli said grimly, and told him what he'd told us.

Brandon's facial expression didn't change, but he blinked a few times. I got the impression he had taken some kind of blow, but he sounded wooden when he spoke. "I'm sorry that that young woman turned up. Her family should have some closure, too, I suppose."

"I suppose," Eli said. "I just can't believe we found her. On the whole ocean floor, what are the odds? It's almost like she wanted us to find her."

I shivered. "The question is, who put her there?"

"It'll be hard solving a case that old," John said.

"And is her murderer still on the island, or was it a summer person?" I wondered.

"She disappeared in June twenty years ago," Eli informed us. "Could be either."

"And the mail boat doesn't have passenger records," I said. "That's too bad."

"You're assuming whoever it was took the mail boat," John said. "The person who did this must have had access to a boat of their own."

"Of course," I said. "They had to get the body and the anchor out to sea." I looked at Eli. "You're sure about the anchor? And the necklace?"

"I'm sure," he said. "I just wish I knew who did it."

"So do I," I said, wondering if someone on Cranberry Island might have been carrying such a dark secret for twenty years.

∼

ELI STOPPED by the Cranberry Island store on the way home to pick up some sweets, which meant the entire island knew what was going on by the time I started prepping dinner.

"Eli says he knows who it was," Charlene said, "but he wouldn't tell me. He did say it was the killick that sat outside the museum. Since that disappeared twenty years ago, it wasn't too hard to figure out who he was thinking of."

"What conclusion did you come to?" I asked.

"Mandy Hoyle. She disappeared one June night and never turned up again; the same night as the killick, as it turns out. No one ever connected the two, but now it makes sense."

"What did people think happened?"

"Oh, everyone said she ran off with a boy from the mainland; she was kind of boy-crazy. But when she didn't turn back up, that theory kind of went cold, and we all figured something bad had happened. There was a whole group of teenagers who hung out together at the time, but no leads."

"Who did she hang with?"

"Tom Lockhart and John, for starters," she said.

"John said he spent some time with her," I said. "Who else?"

"Me," she said, looking at me, tears forming in her eyes. She wiped them away. "Mandy and I were friends; we weren't super close, but we hung out together sometimes. We liked to hunt for sea glass together, and she and I both smoked our first cigarette down below the pier at low tide." A wistful smile passed over her face, and her eyes were unfocused. "I still think about her sometimes," she said quietly. "I was hoping she was off living a good life somewhere, but..." She trailed off.

I squeezed her shoulder. "I'm so sorry. That's got to be such a horrible feeling."

"It is," she confirmed. "And the thing was, I have no idea what happened to her. Even now. Only I know for sure it wasn't good."

"No," I agreed, and sat in silence for a moment, keeping my grieving friend company. "Any ideas what might have happened?"

"No," she said. "I wish I did."

"She wasn't involved with anyone at the time, was she?"

"Not that I knew of," Charlene said. "She and Tom went out a few times, but that was earlier... they weren't together anymore. And if she was seeing someone, I think she would have told me. Besides, that kind of thing is hard to hide on an island this size, as you can imagine."

"I can," I said. Word traveled fast, to say the least.

"And now all I can think about is Tania," she said, glancing down at her phone, which was dark. "I still haven't heard from her. What if the same thing happens to her?"

The thought had crossed my mind, too, but I didn't

share that with Charlene. "I'm sure we'll find her," I reassured her, wishing I felt as sure as I sounded. "With Mandy, there weren't any leads; she just disappeared. It's different with Tania. We know she was seeing someone."

"Yeah, but we don't know who," she said. "Maybe he used a fake name! Maybe he lured her somewhere and did horrible things to her..."

"Don't jump to conclusions. It hasn't been long; I'm sure we'll find her," I told Charlene, reaching out to touch her shoulder.

"I just hope she's alive when we do," she said, and a shiver passed through me at her words.

∼

THE REST of the day was quiet and somber—if you exclude the number of phone calls I got fishing for information. I handled dinner myself, as John was busy working with the police on the body—and on trying to track down Tania.

"Horrible news today," Max said when I went out to serve dinner.

The multimillionaire and his entourage were over by the window, going over the new data the research vessel had found, and were evidently completely unfazed by their first view of the underwater graveyard—and of the unexpected body of what was likely to be an innocent young woman.

"I know," I agreed. "She's got family here; it must be a shock."

Max and Ellie were somber and full of questions. "We heard about the body you found," Ellie told me as I put a plate of sole meunière down in front of her. "That's dreadful; it sounds like she was from the island."

"And no one knows what happened," Max chimed in.

"No, they don't," I said. John had told me the mainland police had sent a launch out to the site; I wasn't sure how they were going to deal with a crime scene that was twenty years old and several hundred feet underwater, but fortunately that wasn't my issue to deal with. I did wonder if Eli had stopped by the Hoyles' yet. And if I should swing by with something to comfort them. "It's very sad," I continued. "And now, to top it all off, my friend's niece is missing."

"Oh, no," Max said. "How old is she?"

"She's twenty," I said.

"Almost the same age as my daughters," Max said, shivering. "What happened?"

I told her about the empty cottage, and the shadowy boyfriend nobody had met. "The police are looking for her, but Charlene hasn't heard anything since she vanished. We're trying to stay optimistic."

"But today's discovery's got to be hard," Max said. "Is there anything we can do to help?"

"I wish there were," I said, "but unless you're able to find out who a boyfriend named Dan is, good luck."

"Dan? That's specific."

"I know, right? All we know is that he lives on Mount Desert Island."

"I wish we had access to her phone records," Max said. "Are the police looking into it?"

"I'll ask John," I said.

"Your handsome husband?" she asked.

"Yes," I confirmed. "He's the island deputy, and is pushing the mainland police to search for Tania."

"Did you get a chance to look at her mail?"

"We did a quick search, but didn't turn anything up. It might be worth going back and looking."

"If you need a second pair of eyes..." Max offered.

"Or a third," Ellie chimed in.

"Thanks," I said. "I'll talk to Charlene and let you know."

∼

There was still no word from Tania by the time we closed everything up that night.

"What a day," my husband said as I put up the last clean bowl. "Still nothing from Tania?"

"Not that I've heard. Are they checking her phone records?" I asked John as he refilled the cats' food.

"They are," he said. "I'm hoping we have some answers by tomorrow."

I double-checked to make sure I had everything I needed for tomorrow's breakfast and asked the question that had been plaguing me all day. "Do you think she's going to be okay?"

He grimaced as he sealed up the bag of cat food. "The longer she's gone, the less likely it is, I'm afraid. I just don't know."

"Maybe the phone records will give us at least a lead," I said. "Charlene's had such a bad week; first Tania goes missing, and then she finds out her old friend was murdered twenty years ago. Your friend, too, I hear."

"I knew her," John said. "But I wouldn't say we were friends."

"No?" I asked.

"We just kind of hung out together by default. All of us did... Tom, Charlene, and a couple of other summer people teenagers. The group kind of changed from year to year. Mandy's parents were on the mainland, but she came over to stay with Emmeline in the summer for a few weeks." He sighed. "The nice thing about the island was that it felt safe;

from the time we were little, we could all just roam, and our parents wouldn't have to worry about us.."

"Were there any other disappearances around the same time?"

"No," he said, shaking his head. "Hers was the first and last for a long time, thank goodness."

"How do you investigate something like that?" I asked.

"Well, you talk to the people she was close to at the time, for starters," he said.

"That would include you."

"And Tom Lockhart, and Charlene," John pointed out.

"You won't be suspects, will you?"

"I don't know, Natalie," he said. "So you know, though, Mandy and I did go out briefly, the summer before she disappeared."

"What happened?" I asked, glad he was telling me.

"We weren't a good fit. I broke it off at the end of the summer."

"That must have been awkward."

"It was," he admitted, "but we just didn't talk about it."

"Wow," I said. "All this history I didn't know."

"Yeah," he said.

"And she didn't show up on unsolved cases or anything? It just got dropped?"

"Her parents searched for years. Put up missing-person posters, followed leads, got her on a milk carton... but the trail ran cold. And now we know why."

"Did you talk to Emmeline?"

"I did," he said. "She kind of guessed it, after all this time, but really knowing..." he shook his head. "It's hard."

"It is," I said. "I think I'm going to go back over to her place with Charlene tomorrow. See if we can turn something else up. Have the police been there?"

"Not yet," he said. "I think they're hoping the phone records will give them a lead."

"I hope they do," I said.

And soon.

~

It was a restless night, filled with dreams of sunken anchors and long hair floating deep in the ocean and Tania's voice, staticky and distant, like a long-distance connection that kept breaking up. I woke up once in the middle of the night, thinking I heard someone crying out. I sat up straight; Biscuit and Smudge were both curled into the crook behind John's knees, and John was still sound asleep.

I glanced at the clock—it was 2:33—and waited a few minutes to see if I heard anything else, but there was nothing but the sound of the waves against the shore. After a long while, I lay back and tried to drift off again, still thinking of that dream of Tania, and hoping she hadn't met the same fate as Mandy.

I must have nodded off eventually, because the next time I looked at the clock it was 7:30, and the sun was already flooding the windows with clean, clear morning light. I pulled on a pair of sweatpants and a sweatshirt, thankful to leave last night's dark dreams behind, and headed downstairs, leaving John and the cats snuggled up in bed.

This morning I was making a strata and a batch of muffins for my gluten- and sugar-loving guests, and a frittata for the rest of them. I hadn't seen much of Brandon since the discovery; he and his team had been back and forth from the research vessel and talking excitedly about next steps. As I cracked eggs into a bowl, I wondered about what drove his fascination with the sunken U-Boat. And about his time in Maine.

I had just finished layering bread, cheese, ham and egg and was about to tuck the strata into the oven when there was a light tap on the swinging door to the dining room, and Max peeked through.

"Hey," I said.

"Sorry to bother you," she said, "but I can't get my coffee maker to work. Mind if I beg a cup from you?"

"Come on in!" I said. "There's an almost-full pot on the counter; I just made it a few minutes ago. You're welcome to keep me company if you like. I'm just getting breakfast together."

"Oh, can I?" she asked. "Ellie is still sound asleep, and I could use the company. I kept thinking about that missing girl last night, and my own two girls, and everything else going on in my life."

"I didn't sleep well either," I told her as I put the strata in the oven and reached for the flour canister for the batch of cranberry-walnut muffins I was making to go with the strata, along with a fruit salad. "Where are your two girls?"

"They're both in college," Max told me as she poured herself a cup of coffee and added a lump of sugar.

"Half and half is in the fridge," I informed her.

"Thanks," she said, and reached for the fridge door. "At first, I kept wanting to check on them all the time—you know, call and make sure they made it home, and find out what their schedules were—but I had to learn to trust that they'd be okay. And then I hear about something like this..."

"Are they at the same college?" I asked as she stirred her coffee.

"No," she said, and glanced at my mug. "Want a refill?"

"I'd love one," I said. "With a splash of half and half and a touch of sugar, please," I added as I measured out flour and reached for the baking powder.

"No problem," she said, topping up my coffee, giving it a stir, and setting it down next to the bowl. She walked over to the kitchen table and sat down, taking a sip of her coffee before continuing. "They're twins, but they went completely different directions; one's an electrical engineering major, and the other's a linguistics/poli sci double major. The engineer is at Rensselaer Polytechnic, and the linguistics/poli sci major is at the University of Maine."

"Identical, or fraternal?"

"Fraternal," she said. "Although shouldn't it be sororital or something? I always thought that was silly, since they're girls."

"I'd never thought about that," I said. "How are they handling all the changes?"

"One of them seems okay with it, all things considered. The other... I think she's mad at me. And I don't know what to do about it." Her shoulders slumped. "My husband and I tried for a long time, but things just weren't working. We both still love the kids, and we're both still dedicated parents, but all the change... I know it's hard on them."

"That sounds really difficult," I said as I plopped butter into a bowl and put it in the microwave. "It's still so fresh, too. I'm sure time will help."

"I hope so," she said with a sigh. "But more than that, I hope Charlene finds her niece soon."

"So do I," I said as I pulled the bowl out of the microwave and added orange juice.

Max took another sip of her coffee. "Can I ask you an unrelated question?"

"Shoot."

"You suggested I buy a bookstore of my own. Were you serious?"

I looked up from cracking eggs into another bowl and smiled at Max. "I was," I said. "I'd do the numbers, of course, and make sure it's viable... but if it's what you love to do, then why not?"

"You didn't have any experience with a B&B before you started this place?"

"No," I said, remembering the first time I saw the building I now called home, and how different Cranberry Island was from my longtime home in Austin, Texas. "It just felt... right," I said. "And it really was a gamble. I had no family, no friends... I'd never even been to Maine before. But my soul said 'yes.'"

"And you're glad you listened?"

I thought of John, and Gwen, and my mother-in-law, all of whom had joined me here as family... not to mention Charlene, and Eli, and all the other dear friends I'd made since moving here. I was a part of the island now, and it was a part of me. "I can't imagine what my life would be if I hadn't," I said truthfully.

"Huh," she said, taking another sip of coffee and looking out the window with a faraway look on her face. "Unless Ellie's wrong about Loretta's shop in Snug Harbor—and I hope she is, and Loretta's okay—I have no idea where to even begin. You just walked into this place. All I have is an idea."

"The place will come," I told her as I finished whisking the eggs together with the orange juice and butter, then stirred it into the dry ingredients. "Just stay open to it. If it's meant to be... you'll find it."

Max turned to me. "You think?"

"I do," I said. As the words left my mouth, there was a hammering sound from behind her.

I looked up to see Catherine outside the window of the back door, looking pale and frantic.

I ran to the door and unlocked it. "What's wrong?"

"There's... there's... a body," she gasped. "Next to the carriage house."

6

"Who is it?" I asked, my heart in my throat. Could it be Tania?

"It's a man," Catherine said.

"Thank God it's not Tania, then," Max said, echoing my thoughts.

"No... but I don't know who it is. He's facedown by the apple trees. Someone stuck a knife in him." She shuddered.

"Show me," I said.

"It's right next to the carriage house," she said, her face pale against her pink workout jacket; she must have been going for a morning run when she found him. "I don't want to look at him again, though."

"You don't have to," I said. "Why don't you go wake John up, and I'll see if I can identify the body."

"Can I come?" Max asked as Catherine headed for the stairs to our rooms above the kitchen.

"Sure," I said. "I could use a little moral support."

I slipped on the shoes I kept by the back door and headed out to the back deck. It was a beautiful morning, the air crisp and clear, the water an impossible blue, the apple trees heavy with red fruit. I steeled myself for what I'd find beneath them.

Together Max and I hurried down the path to the carriage house. "Two bodies in two days. Does this happen often?" she asked.

"More often than I'd like," I admitted. As I spoke, I caught a glimpse of legs in the emerald green grass. "There he is," I said as we slowed down, being careful not to get too close; it was, after all, a crime scene.

"Do you recognize him?" she asked when the full body was in view. As Catherine said, it was a man, and his face was turned toward us, half-covered by leaves. I could make out his five-o-clock shadow, and the receding hairline of a man in middle age. He had a look of surprise on his face, and as Catherine had said, what looked like a kitchen knife protruded from his back. The fabric of his shirt was stained dark red.

"I think I do," I said. "It's Steve Batterly. He does odd jobs for some of the wealthy folks who come for the summer. He lives on the other side of the island, though; I can't think why he's here."

"There's something in his hand," Max said, craning to look. "A piece of paper, it looks like."

I took a step to the right, trying to make out what was on it. "It's a handwritten note. Something something opportunity, maybe?"

"Not much of an opportunity," Max said. "Do you think someone lured him here so they could kill him?"

"That's my guess," I said. "The question is, who?"

"And why?" Max added, her face grim.

As she spoke, John and Catherine hurried up behind us.

"It's Steve Batterly," I informed him.

"What is he doing here?" John asked, echoing my own thoughts.

"There's a note in his hand with something about an opportunity on it. I'm guessing someone lured him here and then killed him."

"Stabbed him in the back, no less. Looks like a kitchen knife; nothing special."

"The kind of thing you could buy at any store," I said. "It would be so much easier if it was a monogrammed pen knife."

"It never is," John said.

Catherine stood a little ways away, looking toward the water; she was still pale, and her hand was at her throat, her arm wrapped tight around her body. "I can't believe this happened right outside where I was sleeping. What if it was me? I go out by myself all the time. What if someone was just a serial killer, waiting for the first victim? What if they were still there when I went out for my run?"

"I don't think this was random," John assured her. "I think someone lured him here intentionally. But I'll join you on your morning runs for a while, until we get this figured out."

"Thank you," she said, shooting him a look of relief and gratitude.

"Why stab him?" Max asked, considering the body. A few golden apple tree leaves had settled on his body.

"Quieter than a gun," John said. "Did you hear anything last night?"

"No," Catherine said, "but I've been using a CPAP machine the last year or so, and it's so noisy I don't hear much."

"I heard something," I said. "Around 2:30 this morning. I thought I must have dreamed it, so I went back to sleep."

"What did you hear?"

"Kind of a scream," I said, realizing I'd probably heard Steve crying out as the knife went into his back.

"That will help with time of death, potentially. I've called the mainland police," he said. "I'm guessing we'll be hearing from Gertrude of the Daily Mail at any moment now."

"One of these days I'm going to ask her to write something nice about the inn," I said. Gertrude was not my favorite reporter, to say the least; I sometimes thought the Gray Whale Inn survived despite her.

"Good luck with that," John said. "That woman's got it in for us."

I wasn't sure he was right, but I had to admit it sure seemed so.

"I guess even in paradise, there's trouble," Max said.

"There is," I said. "But we always pull through." I looked at John, who was looking handsome even in his plaid pajama pants and green waffle-weave Henley, his sandy hair tousled.

"We do," he concurred, and reached for my hand.

∽

I WENT BACK INSIDE to finish making breakfast; the kitchen smelled marvelous. The strata was almost ready to come out of the oven, and the batter just needed the addition of cranberries and walnuts before I started scooping it into muffin tins and sprinkling it with turbinado sugar. I'd keep the strata warm on top of the stove, covering it with a tea towel, while the muffins baked.

Max joined me, refilling her coffee and sitting back down at the kitchen table as I measured out the berries and nuts for the batter.

"What do you know about the man who died?" she asked.

"I know he worked odd jobs around the island," I said. "A lot of people do. He's..." I corrected myself. "He was a handyman. I had him here once, but I didn't like him much. I never hired him again."

"What do you mean?"

"I hired him to fix the front door a few years ago; it kept popping open. He kept asking a lot of questions about how much the place had cost me," I told her, "and once I found him looking through the papers on the front desk."

"Did you fire him?"

"I let him finish the job," I said, "but I never hired him again, that's for sure."

"So he's nosy," she said.

"Maybe he was too nosy," I suggested as I put muffin cups into the tins. "Maybe he found out something he shouldn't have."

"Where was he working?" she asked.

"I know he's worked for Murray Selfridge—he's a local developer type who used to date my mother-in-law—but lately he's been helping out on a remodeling job for the Jamesons, I hear."

"Think he might have dug up too much dirt on one of them?" she asked.

"I'm not sure Murray would care, frankly," I said. "I don't really know anything about Steve. But he's been on the island for years and has worked for all kinds of people. He could have dug up dirt on anyone." I thought about it for a moment. "But you do have a point. For someone to kill him now, he would have had to find something out recently."

"Exactly," she said.

"It's still a big assumption, though. I really don't know anything about him."

"Maybe a jilted lover?"

"If anyone will know, it's Charlene," I said. I glanced at the clock; it was still before eight. A bit early for my friend, I knew, but she always liked to be the first to know about goings-on, so I knew she wouldn't mind the call. "I'll ask right now," I said. "As soon as I get these muffins in, anyway." I sprinkled sugar over the tops of the muffins and slid them into the oven, then refilled my coffee and dialed Charlene.

"Do you have news on Tania?" she asked as soon as she picked up.

"Not yet, unfortunately," I said, and I could practically feel her deflate on the other end of the line. "But Catherine found Steve Batterly next to the carriage house with a knife in him."

"No way," she said, then, "Oh, no."

"What?"

"Tom Lockhart threatened to kill him just two days ago, in front of half the island."

7

"What? Why?" I asked.

"I don't know," she said. "But he told him to stop mucking around in things and said if he ever set foot on his property or said another word about him, he'd make sure it was the last thing he ever did."

"Ouch," I said. "Why?"

"I don't know," she said. "Steve had a bit of a reputation for digging up dirt on people and stirring up trouble. I have no idea why people continued to hire him."

"Maybe he blackmailed them into it?" I said, half-jokingly.

"I can't think why else they'd have him," she replied darkly. "Although from what I hear, he does do good work."

"He did a good job on my front door, but I didn't like him at all," I said.

"What kind of knife?" Charlene asked.

"I don't think I'm supposed to say," I said. "But the wound was definitely not self-inflicted." I glanced out toward the carriage house, where I knew John was keeping watch over the body. "The mainland police are on their way."

"Maybe you can ask them if they have any news on Tania," she suggested.

"Of course I will. I was talking with Max about the situation, and she suggested we go take a closer look at Tania's place. See if maybe there's something we missed that might tell us who her mystery man is."

"I was thinking that, too. Are you free this morning?"

"Once I get through being questioned by the police, I'm all yours," I said. "How are you doing with the whole Mandy thing?"

"I'm shaken up, but I'm more worried about Tania."

"Of course," I said, gathering the bowls I'd used and putting them in the sink. "I didn't know Mandy and John were a thing for a while," I said. "He'd never mentioned her before."

"He dated all kinds of girls; they all fell for him," Charlene said.

"But not you?"

"Not me," she said. "He's handsome, all right, but there was never any chemistry between us."

"Thank heavens for that," I said. Charlene definitely had me in the looks department.

"Do you want to meet at Tania's at ten?" she asked.

"That'll work for me," I said.

"I hope we find something," Charlene said. "And when we're done, I'm going to go over to the inn and grill those detectives, or whatever they are, and tell them to find my girl."

~

BY THE TIME breakfast rolled around, the detectives had arrived and were gathering evidence and Brandon and his entourage were ensconced at a corner table with a view of the proceedings—or what they could see, anyway, since the carriage house hid the body from view.

"What happened?" Rebecca asked, eyes wide. She was dressed, as usual, in a conservative pin-striped blue-and-white blouse with tan slacks, her hair and make-up understated but immaculate. She reminded me a little of Catherine, at least sartorially.

"There was a death last night," I said. "Someone from the island; no one associated with the inn."

"Died?" Antoine asked, his eyes alight with interest for the first time since he'd seen the sunken sub. "How?"

"That's what they're investigating," I said as I put an egg-white frittata filled with veggies in front of him.

"Natural causes?" he pressed.

"Ah... no," I said.

"That explains the police presence," he said, ignoring the omelet and staring at me with curiosity.

"Are we safe?" Brandon asked in a mild voice.

"I can't think why not," I said. "I think the location was just unfortunate."

"What if there's some crazy killer out there?" Rebecca said, then turned to Antoine. "Maybe we should move over to the mainland."

"The police said there's not a serial killer," I said, echoing what John had said earlier. He was, after all, the island deputy. "I don't think you have anything to worry about."

"How did he—it's a he?" the bodyguard asked.

I nodded.

"How did he die?"

"I don't think I'm allowed to say," I said.

"I'm going to go take a look," Antoine said in a tone of voice that did not invite debate. He shoved back his chair, stood up from the table and headed for the back door. With his broad shoulders and barrel chest, he looked... well, menacing. Dangerous, really. Dangerous enough to put a knife in someone's back? I wondered briefly. Maybe to protect his rich boss?

I didn't bother trying to stop Antoine—I could tell it wouldn't make any difference—and trusted the investigators would make sure they had the space they needed.

"Are you sure we're safe?" Rebecca asked again.

"I'm sure," I said. The murderer couldn't be staying at the inn, after all, could they? No one here had any connection to the island. Except Brandon, I remembered, looking at him with new curiosity. Why had he chosen to stay on Cranberry Island instead of the mainland—or on his own yacht?

I excused myself and wandered over to the other side of the dining room, where Max and Ellie were enjoying the strata. After all the stress this morning, I'd helped myself to a bit of strata, too, along with a few muffins. Thank goodness for elastic waistbands.

"How are you this morning?" I asked Ellie.

"Curious," Ellie said. "Do the police have any idea what happened?"

"I haven't heard anything new yet," I said.

"Thank goodness it's not Tania," Ellie breathed. "Not that it's not horrible."

"Did you hear anything last night?" I asked.

"I slept like a baby," Ellie said, and turned to Max. "You?"

"I didn't hear a thing," she said.

"Are you still going over to Tania's place today?" Ellie asked.

"I am," I said.

"I'm happy to be another set of eyes if you like," she said.

"I've got two daughters of my own; I'd love to help in any way I can. Actually," she said, "is Tania on social media?"

"She is, but Charlene said she hasn't been posting."

"If she knows what her account names are, we can look to see if she's posted anything."

"Why didn't I think of that?" I asked.

"That's the only way I know what my kids are up to," Max said, rolling her eyes.

"I'll check with her and let you know," I said. "Be right back."

∼

Charlene was at the door to the kitchen fifteen minutes later, phone in hand, dark rings around her eyes and her caramel-streaked hair pulled back into a messy ponytail. She wore a U Maine sweatshirt and sweatpants, and looked as if she hadn't slept in three days. Which she probably hadn't.

"Where is she?" she asked.

"Still at breakfast," I said.

"Think she'd mind if I joined her?"

"Not at all," I said. "I'll go with you."

"Hey" Max said, standing up as my friend hurried up to their table. "I'm so sorry to hear about Tania. I hope we can help you figure out where your girl is!"

"Me too," Charlene said, pulling up a chair.

"Do you want some strata, or a muffin?" I offered.

"No," Charlene said, very uncharacteristically. "I can't eat right now."

"I'll get you coffee then," I said, and as Max and Charlene hunched over her phone, I poured a cup of dark coffee with cream and two sugars. As I returned to the table, I glanced over at Brandon's entourage. Antoine was back, eating his strata mechanically, and Rebecca was on her cell phone, speaking urgently. I heard something about "public relations liability" and "National Geographic" before I set Charlene's mug down in front of her.

"She posted on her Instagram account half an hour ago," Charlene said excitedly. "Look!" She showed me a picture of a path into dark woods with the hashtag #roadlesstraveled. Although I was glad to see some sign of activity from Tania, something about the photo—and the caption—was unsettling.

"Can you tell where the picture was taken?" I asked.

"She didn't list it, but I'll bet there's a way to tell; I think it's encoded in the photo somehow."

"We should tell John," I said.

"This doesn't really look like Tania's typical posts," Charlene said, scrolling through a series of filtered selfies.

"Wait," I said, stopping her at a photo from two weeks ago that showed someone's arm—male, by the size of it—around her. "Can you blow that one up?"

"Sure," she said, magnifying the photo. "What's that ring?" I asked, pointing to a gold ring with a crest on the hand draped over her shoulder.

"I can't tell," she said, and looked up at me. "Do you have a computer we can look at this on?"

"I do," I said. "It's in the front office."

"Natalie?" It was Rebecca.

"I'll be right back," I told Charlene. "If you'll e-mail or text the photo to me, I can blow it up on the screen," I said.

"Will do," Charlene said as I headed over to the millionaire's table.

"What can I do for you?" I asked. Brandon was busy on a tablet and didn't look up.

"I've got a few news agencies that are coming out to cover the discovery," she said. "Can you keep this situation" —she flicked a manicured hand toward the police next to the carriage house— "hush-hush? We don't want it to detract from the magnitude of what Mr. Marks and his team have found."

"I don't know exactly how I'm going to keep it hush-hush," I said, "but I'm not going to be advertising it, if that helps. When are these folks arriving? Will they need rooms?"

"In light of what's going on out there," she said, her eyes flicking to the carriage house again, "we thought it best to suggest they stay elsewhere."

Wonderful.

"Right," I said shortly. "Well, let me know if you need anything else."

"We will, actually," she said. "Could you put together a gluten-free bag lunch? We'll need it within the hour."

"I'll see what I can do," I said, and excused myself to the front desk, trying to resist the urge to sprinkle the lunch I was about to make with extra bread flour. Assuming I had something I could whip up into an impromptu gluten-free lunch, that was. I was going to be charging extra on their bill, that was for sure.

"Did you e-mail the picture to me?" I asked Charlene.

"I did," Charlene said.

I went into my office and pulled up my inbox; sure enough, there was the photo. I saved it, then opened the file.

"Can you make it bigger?" Charlene asked.

"I can," I said, magnifying the image. "Can you see what's on the ring?"

"It's some kind of shield, or coat of arms, it looks like," Charlene said.

"Maybe some kind of school ring?" Max suggested.

"Probably," I said. "It's got a number on it, looks like. Let's print it and show it to John; I'll e-mail it to him, too, so he can share it with the police on the mainland." I hit PRINT. "Why don't you guys see what else you can turn up on her accounts? I've got to make a few box lunches, and then we can head over to Tania's place."

"Sounds like a plan," Charlene said. "What other social media apps don't I know about?" she asked Max as I hurried back to the kitchen to try to come up with something gluten-free to send with the entourage.

Fortunately, I'd made some quinoa the day before, planning to use it in a salad. I grabbed it from the fridge, added a can of chickpeas and some feta, along with lemon juice, olive oil, garlic salt, chopped-up cucumber and a box of cherry tomatoes. I nipped out the back to get some fresh basil from the pot I kept on the back porch during the day (I took it in when it got too cold); as I harvested some leaves, I watched as two young officers moved a body bag to a stretcher.

"John!" I called, seeing my husband standing a few feet away from the proceedings, his face grim.

He strode over to meet me, and I told him what we'd discovered about Tania. "I think there's usually GPS info encoded into Instagram photos," I said. "Plus, one of the photos has someone's arm around her; there's a ring in the picture. We blew it up and printed it."

"Good thinking," he said.

"It was Max," I said. "She's got college-age daughters; it was her idea."

"Frankly, you'd think the detectives would have gone that route," John said.

"You don't think they're taking it seriously?"

"Either that or they're understaffed," he suggested. "I'll get this info to them right away. If she posted that picture yesterday, she may still be there."

"I hope so," I said, my eyes drifting over to the body bag. I hoped Tania wouldn't find her way into one, I thought with a shiver. Then my mind went back to the note I'd spotted in Steve's hand. Why had someone lured him to the inn, rather than somewhere else on the island?

"Any more clues?" I asked.

"Just the note in his hand," John said. "At least that's all I know about. They may find something else when they do the autopsy."

I shivered at the thought.

"I'm going to go to Tania's with Charlene in a bit. I'm making box lunches for the multimillionaire and his entourage; I'll take care of the kitchen before I go."

"Thanks," he said, giving me a kiss. "I'm sorry I'm tied up."

"It's no problem," I said. "I understand. I've got this."

"Thanks. I love you," he said.

"Love you too," I said, feeling my heart melt a little as he kissed my forehead and then hurried back to the knot of police officers next to the carriage house. I watched him go, then plucked another stem of basil and retreated to the kitchen.

It only took ten minutes to finish whipping up the quinoa salad and spooning it into tubs. I put the tubs into three brown bags, and then added a few of the gluten-free chocolate meringues I'd whipped up the day before to each bag, along with an apple and a bottle of water. Not too bad for ten minutes notice, I thought with satisfaction as I delivered the bags to the trio in the dining room.

They accepted the bags without comment.

"Will you be here for dinner?" I asked.

"We won't know until later," Rebecca informed me.

"Please let me know by four, so I can plan," I said.

She nodded, then looked back at her phone, essentially dismissing me.

I'd be charging a LOT more for those box lunches, I thought as I gathered the rest of the dishes and took them to the kitchen. I did a quick clean-up before returning to find Charlene, Max, and Ellie still huddled over my computer at the front desk.

"Find anything else?" I asked.

"Nothing yet," she said. "I think she's got a Snapchat account, but I can't get into it, and besides, those photos don't last."

"I told John about the Instagram post; he's going to have the folks on the mainland see if they can get GPS coordinates on that photo," I said.

"You're the best," Charlene said, looking more hopeful than I'd seen her in days. "Ready to go to Tania's?"

"Mind if we go with you?" Max offered.

"I'd love the extra eyes," Charlene said, then turned to me. "Can we take the van?"

"Of course."

I had just finished clearing the last of the dishes and put on my jacket to head out when my phone rang; it was Lorraine Lockhart.

"Hey, Lorraine. What's up?" I asked.

"Oh, Natalie... I need your help."

"What? Why?"

"They... the police came and they arrested Tom!"

8

"What? Why?"

"Steve Batterly... I know you know someone stabbed him outside the inn," she said. "Well, apparently there was some kind of note in the guy's hand, and the knife in his back..." She swallowed. "I... I think it came from my kitchen. I'm with the kids at Claudette and Eli's right now; the police are searching the house for evidence."

"Oh, Lorraine," I said. "I'll be right over."

"What's wrong?" Charlene asked as I hung up the phone.

"The police arrested Tom for killing Steve," I said.

"They didn't waste any time at all, did they? Why?"

I told her what Lorraine had told me.

"That makes no sense at all!" she said. "Tom barely had anything to do with Steve!"

"They've known each other a long time... maybe it had something to do with an old grudge?" I had another thought. "Were Tom and Mandy ever an item?"

Charlene shook her head. "Not that I know of. Oh... you're thinking maybe Tom thought Steve killed Mandy?"

"Or that the police think that," I said.

"Tom would never do anything like that," Charlene said. "And there's no way he'd do anything to jeopardize your inn."

"I'm not saying he did," I said. "I'm just trying to understand why he was arrested."

"Poor Lorraine," Charlene said.

"I know."

"Whoever killed Steve, it wasn't Tom. We've got to figure out who did it."

I sighed. Tania missing, Tom arrested, an old disappearance that turned out to be murder... it was shaping up to be one heck of a bad week.

∽

Charlene, Max and Ellie headed off to Tania's without me; I was going to head to Claudette and Eli's to check on Lorraine. As Charlene pulled out of the driveway, I pulled an emergency loaf of banana bread out of the freezer. John came in as I was searching for my sneakers, and when I told him the news, he was as shocked as I was.

"They arrested Tom without telling me?"

"Did you have any idea they would?"

"I know there were initials on the note in Steve's hand," he said. "T.L. But I had no idea they were making an arrest."

"Speaking of notes; what idiot would sign a note with his or her initials, kill someone, and then leave the note in his hand?"

"It seems crazy, I know, but people do dumb things when adrenaline gets involved. And if they can confirm the knife came from the Lockharts' house..."

"Even if it did, that doesn't prove anything. Everyone on this island leaves their doors unlocked," I countered.

"I know that, but all the evidence points to Tom, and they're so short-staffed I'm afraid they're not inclined to look further. As far as they're concerned, I get the feeling it's an open-and-shut case."

"What's the motive?"

"Someone told them they saw them arguing the other day. The theory is that Steve was blackmailing Tom, and Tom was trying to tempt him with dirt on Brandon so that he could kill him off."

"Wonderful," I said. "Where did they come up with this theory?"

"Tom told him to stay out of his business or he'd be sorry, evidently."

"I heard that, too. Charlene said he threatened him in front of the whole island the other day. Someone must have told the police. What do you know about Steve?" I asked.

"I just know he does odd jobs around the island, and has lived in the house he inherited from his grandparents for the last twenty years. He drives a nice car, though, and has an expensive boat."

"Family money?"

"Maybe," he said, shrugging. "Maybe it's because he doesn't have any housing costs."

"Maybe," I said. "Or maybe he was picking up extra money by blackmailing people. After all, didn't that note offer some dirt on Brandon?"

"How do you know that?" John asked. "You didn't touch anything, did you?"

"Of course not! I could see it in his hand," I said. "I didn't see the initials at the bottom, though." I thought about it for a moment. "I know he worked as a handyman... who did he work for?"

"He works for the Karstadts and the Jamesons, mainly," he said. "He also does a lot of odd jobs for Murray."

"The one time he was here I found him snooping in the office," I commented. "What if he used his access to people's houses as an opportunity to find incriminating evidence, then used it against them?"

"Why should they still keep him around and pay him, then?"

"If the alternative was exposure, they might."

"And the blackmail money would be a good source of extra income," John admitted. "Plus, doing odd jobs, it would explain his income."

"If he took the hush-hush payments under the table, it would be tax-free, too. Any way to get our hands on his tax returns?"

"Not legally," John said.

I cocked an eyebrow.

"No," he said flatly.

"Even if the front door is open?"

"No," he repeated.

I sighed. "If he was blackmailing people, we've got to find out who. If we can at least establish motives for other people, then maybe we can help defend Tom, if not get him off the hook."

"You're convinced he's innocent?" John asked.

I gave him a look. "Are you?"

"I hope he is," he said, in a tone of voice that made me wonder.

"What exactly would he be blackmailing Tom for? Lorraine knows about the affair he had some years back."

"I don't know," he said. "What if that wasn't the only one he had?"

"You think?" I asked.

He sighed. "I saw him with a woman I didn't recognize over in Northeast Harbor the other day. She was attractive, and they seemed... well, intimate."

"Oh, no," I groaned. "Poor Lorraine."

"I don't know if there's anything to it," John said quickly. "But it made me wonder."

"I hope there's nothing to it," I said, feeling sick to my stomach. "I'm headed over to see Lorraine now. Apparently the police are going over the house with a fine-tooth comb, so Lorraine and the kids are camping out at Claudette and Eli's place. I'm just going to bring some banana bread."

"Don't mention what I saw on the mainland," John asked.

"Of course not," I said. "I'm just going to comfort her."

"What's the dinner plan tonight, by the way?"

"Brandon and his entourage don't know if they're here for dinner yet; I told them I need to know by four. I presume Max and Ellie are eating at the inn."

"I like them," John said.

"I do, too. Max has been a big help to Charlene. Let me know what the police find out on that location, by the way, will you? And the sooner, the better; I have a bad feeling about whoever Tania's with."

"Me too," John said. I gave him a quick kiss, then headed to the van.

∼

Lorraine looked like she'd had all the blood drained out of her when I arrived at Claudette and Eli's. Claudette, thankfully, was looking more like her old stolid self; the treatments seemed to be working. She'd set Lorraine up with a cup of tea and a scone, and the kids were in the back yard with Eli, clambering in and out of the boats he kept there while he supervised.

Charlene and I settled ourselves across from Lorraine as Claudette took the banana bread to the kitchen to slice and put out on a plate.

"I'm so sorry about this," I said. "I just told John; he didn't even know."

"I don't understand why!" she said, hugging herself and rocking back and forth. "Tom had nothing to do with Steve. He never liked him, anyway."

"So you have no idea of any way they were connected?"

"Oh, Steve was always trying to wheedle money out of people. Threatened to turn Adam in for fishing extra traps if he didn't give him a few lobsters a week. Unfortunately for Steve, Adam fishes by the book; there wasn't any truth to it."

"Anyone else he went after?"

"Not that I know of," she said, "but anyone who was regular on the island knew to steer clear of him. The only people who would hire him were summer people; everyone else knew better."

"Murray Selfridge hired him."

"That's true," Lorraine acknowledged. "I don't know why. And I'm not sure how you'd blackmail Murray; he's not married, and doesn't have any family I know of."

"Maybe something illegal?" I suggested. "Anyway, I know Steve worked for Murray and a few of the wealthy summer families, but who else did he do jobs for?"

"I saw him coming down the drive from the Jamesons' the other day," Lorraine said, "but to be honest, I didn't pay him much attention. He was just someone to avoid, as far as I was concerned."

"Did he have any relationships that you know of?"

"Why are you asking me all these questions?" she asked, hugging a pillow. "Do you think you can figure out who did it?"

"I can try," I said. "I'm open to any and all ideas."

"If you can, I'll be forever grateful," Lorraine said, glancing out the window to where her children were pretending to row a skiff. "I can't imagine them growing up without their dad."

"I'll do my best," I said.

Lorraine took a sip of her tea, but ignored the scones—and the banana bread Claudette placed on the table between us. As Claudette poured tea for Charlene and me, she nodded toward the moist, dark bread. "This is Emmeline's recipe, isn't it?" Claudette asked.

"It is," I said. "Not sugar-free, though."

"Times like this, that stuff doesn't matter," Claudette said, settling into her chair and retrieving a giant skein of gray yarn and some enormous knitting needles. She looked at Charlene as her needles began to clack. "I hear Tania's missing; I'm so sorry to hear it."

"She is," Charlene said.

"Any word?"

"We've got a new lead," Charlene said, "but we're waiting for the police to see if they can find out where she might have been last."

"An Instagram post," I supplied.

"A what?" Claudette asked.

"I know," I said. "It's a social media platform. I'm learning, too."

"Well, whatever it is, I hope it pans out. She's a good egg."

"Can I use your rest room?" Charlene asked as she set down her tea cup.

"Of course; down the hall to the left," Claudette advised her.

"By the way, have you talked to Emmeline yet?" I asked.

"I have," Claudette said. "It's a shock, after all these years, but I think she's known. In a way, it's good to have some closure."

"Do they have any ideas who it might have been?"

"No," Claudette said. "All she said was that she was going out with some friends. And then she never came back."

This was the first I'd heard of friends. "Did she say which friends?"

"No," Claudette said. "But most of those folks are still on the island." Like John, I thought. And Tom.

Lorraine didn't miss that, either. "Next thing you know they'll be accusing Tom of killing Mandy."

"What?" I asked; all of our heads swiveled to Lorraine.

"Why would they do that?" Charlene asked.

"It seems Tom dated her before she disappeared. Of course, he went out with every other woman on the island, too," she said bitterly, "so that's not a huge surprise."

"Was he one of the friends she was supposed to go out with that night, do you know?"

Lorraine shook her head. "I have no idea. He's never talked about her, or what happened to her. Even when they found the killick and her necklace, he didn't say anything. I only know they dated because Emmeline told me once."

"I'll tell John to talk to Emmeline about the night Mandy disappeared," I said. "Maybe she'll know more. I'm sure she wants to know what happened to her niece."

"It's been a crappy week," Lorraine said, and sank back into the couch.

"We'll do everything we can to help," I promised, but I kept thinking of what John had said.

Was Tom innocent?

Or had he done the unspeakable, and killed Steve Batterly right outside the inn?

9

It was afternoon by the time I made it back to the inn. The police had cleared the area next to the carriage house, and Catherine was sitting at the kitchen table with a mug of tea, looking worried.

"Any word on Tania?" she asked as I walked into the kitchen.

"Some leads, but nothing concrete, at least not yet," I said as I closed the kitchen door behind me. "How are you doing?"

"I'm not too good, to be honest," she said. "That man was murdered practically on my doorstep."

"You know it was Steve, right?"

"I do. And I hear they arrested Tom Lockhart for it." A shudder passed through her thin body. "I can't imagine Tom doing something like that, even though I never liked Steve."

"Did you know him?" I asked.

"He did odd jobs around Murray's place, but always gave me this kind of knowing look. I never cared for him, but Murray said he did good work and wouldn't get rid of him."

"Interesting," I said, pulling up a chair across from her. "I was wondering if Steve might have been blackmailing—or trying to blackmail—islanders. Do you have any idea if Murray might have kept him around because he had some secrets he didn't want getting out?"

Catherine pursed her lips and looked to the side, thinking. "Murray was very sweet to me—at least until the end—but I always got the impression he was a pretty ruthless person when it came to business. Money trumped just about everything else. But I'm not sure he'd care if anyone knew about it."

"If he'd done something illegal, though, and Steve found out about it. Do you think Murray might bend the rules a bit if he needed to?"

"Oh, I'm sure he would," Catherine said. "But he'd always have a way to show he'd used a loophole, at least from what I can see. It's possible, though. He didn't tell me everything about his business dealings."

"Who else did Steve work for, that you know of? I know he was with the Jameson and Karstadt families. Anyone else?"

"Why?" she asked.

I sighed. "I told you they arrested Tom Lockhart for murder today. I'm trying to figure out who might have wanted to kill Steve Batterly."

Catherine narrowed her eyes. "So you think Murray might have... well... killed him?"

"I don't know," I said. "I hope not, but..."

"He's still angry at me," she said. "That would explain doing it next to my cottage; he'd know it would upset me."

"But is he capable of murder?" I asked.

"I wish I could say I knew he wasn't," Catherine said, a sad look on her fine-boned face. She took another sip of her tea and looked out to where she'd found Steve's body that morning. "But who can say for sure?"

"Is there any way you could talk to him?" I asked.

Her face turned stony. "I haven't talked with him in three months."

"I know," I said. "I can go talk to him... I shouldn't have asked."

She took a mechanical sip from her mug, then put it down again. "No," she told me. "I'll do it. It's been a long time coming, anyway."

"You're not going to ask him outright, are you?" I asked.

"Of course not!" she said. "I'll just come by to offer him sympathy for the loss of his handyman. But first, I'm going to get cleaned up."

She was already impeccably dressed, as usual, in slacks and a cashmere twinset, but I just smiled. "Want company?" I asked on a whim.

"Actually," she said, "I could use moral support. Do you have maybe some cookies we can bring as a condolence gift? It seems rather odd, since it was just his handyman, but still... I need an excuse for showing up."

"I've got a dozen sugar cookies left in the freezer," I said, reflecting that my freezer trove was going to need refilling after today.

"If you'll plate them, I'll go get ready," she told me. "The rooms are done, by the way. I found something kind of odd in one of them, though... I didn't know if I should say anything."

"What is it?"

"They're gone all day, right?" she asked. When I confirmed it, she said, "Come look."

I followed her out of the kitchen, through the dining area and the parlor, once again feeling that sense of satisfaction at what I'd created. I really did hope Max found a bookstore to call her own... and made it her own.

Brandon's room was on the second floor, at the end of the hall. Catherine unlocked the door; a moment later we were in the inn's biggest and most luxurious suite, the Crow's Nest.

There was no sign of occupation, except for the chargers on the desk; not a single personal item graced any of the surfaces. Even the big bathroom was sterile, except for a small, neatly zipped toiletries kit on the countertop.

"How did you find anything at all in here?" I asked.

"It was on the floor," she said. "I found it when I was making the bed." She bent down and retrieved a photo—she hadn't moved it, apparently—and handed it to me.

It was an old photo, with a bent corner and that reddish tinge that older pictures get, but the building in the background was immediately recognizable: it was Charlene's store. And in front of it was a gaggle of teenagers, most of whom looked familiar.

"That's Charlene," I said, pointing to a stunning, long-haired younger version of my friend, dressed in a halter top and shorts.

"And John," Catherine said, pointing out my handsome now-husband, looking impossibly young in jeans and a faded green T-shirt, his sandy hair glinting in the sun.

"Is that Tom Lockhart?" I asked, pointing to a lanky boy in running shorts and a hoodie. His arm was slung around the shoulders of a young woman I didn't recognize.

"It is," she said. "And that's Mandy," she informed me, pointing at the red-haired girl. I could see something glinting just above her sternum; no doubt the necklace we'd found next to the sunken U-boat. My heart twisted... the young woman in the picture, full of life, had no idea how short her days were to be.

"Who are these other people, though?" I asked.

"That's Steve Batterly," she said, pointing to a surly-looking dark-haired boy on the other side of Mandy. He looked... disgruntled, somehow. While the other faces were bright with smiles, his mouth turned down, and his eyebrows were knitted together.

"He didn't change much, did he?" I asked, then pointed to three other faces: one girl, and two boys. "Who are these folks?"

"I don't recognize them," she said. "Maybe Charlene will know."

"And this person?" I asked. In the back, there was a half-visible face; whoever it was wore a ball cap with a sports logo on it.

"I don't know," she said.

"Why does he have this?" I asked.

"I have no idea," she said. "Maybe it was left here by an earlier guest?"

"I don't think so. The last people in this room were a retired couple from Minnesota, and before that a family from Barcelona; I would have found anything they left when I was cleaning up, anyway. I wish I could make a copy of this."

"Take a photo," she said.

"Good idea. Then I can show it to Charlene. Although considering they just found Mandy, I'm not sure this is going to be good for Tom's case."

"You think they're going to try to get him for Mandy's murder, too?" Catherine asked.

"Why not?" I said. "They've already got him down for one

murder, after less than a day of investigating. This way they can close two cases at once."

"They wouldn't do that, would they?"

"I hope not," I said as I snapped a few shots of the old photo in my hand, my eyes drawn yet again to Tom's arm around young Mandy's shoulder.

And then a terrible thought occurred to me.

What if Steve knew Tom had killed Mandy?

And what if the discovery of Mandy's body led Tom to get rid of the only person who knew he'd done it?

I pushed the thought away, but there was something in it that wouldn't leave me alone. I hated to think that the head of the lobster co-op and father of young children might be a murderer. But coincidences made me suspicious.

I took one last picture of the snapshot and then gave it back to Catherine, who tucked it back under the bed.

Speaking of coincidences... what was Brandon doing with an old photo of Cranberry Island?

I had a feeling there was more to the reclusive multimillionaire than met the eye.

10

Murray's house was just like Murray: flashy, but without a lot of taste. His Jaguar was parked in the porte-cochere (although why anyone would need a porte-cochere on Cranberry Island was beyond me) when Catherine and I arrived. I left the van in one of the parking spots down the driveway and turned to my mother-in-law.

"Ready?"

She nodded, clutching the plate of cookies in her lap, and took a deep breath. "Let's go," she said.

I followed her up the driveway to the massive front door, admiring, as usual, her sartorial acumen. She'd kept the slacks, but traded in the cashmere twinset for a lovely blue silk blouse that brought out the color of her eyes, and her blonde hair shone in the bright fall sunshine.

She stepped up and pressed the doorbell, drawing herself up into a regal posture Queen Elizabeth would have approved of. It was only a few seconds before the door swung open. It was Murray, looking disheveled in sweatpants and a too-tight Patriots T-shirt that exposed about two inches of belly.

Not for the first time, I wondered how Catherine and Murray had ever been an item.

"Oh... sorry," he said, tugging at his T-shirt. "I wasn't expecting company. Come in, come in," he said, as if he and Catherine hadn't gone through a rather explosive breakup not too long ago.

"Have a seat," he said, leading us to his palatial living room, which looked rather like a set labeled "Men's Smoking Room" from a period film. "Let me change out of these clothes... I was just, uh, working out."

As Catherine perched on the edge of a massive leather wing chair, Murray scuttled out of sight. I'd never seen him look so uncomfortable in all the years I'd known him. It was obvious he still had a crush on Catherine, and as I looked at her, sitting on that massive chair like a princess in pale blue, I could see why.

As we waited for Murray, I looked around the room, which was paneled in dark wood and smelled faintly of cigars. An oil painting with a gaggle of formally dressed and heavily armed men on horses graced the mantle above the giant stone fireplace; it looked like it could have been lifted from any of a number of English country houses. Flanking the fireplace were two massive bookshelves filled with the kind of hardbound books you buy because they look good, not because you want to read them. The head of a buck loomed over us from the wall behind the studded leather couch on which I had deposited myself. The only things that obviously came from this century were a stack of well-thumbed *GQ* and *Esquire* magazines and a book titled *Love Languages*. Was he perhaps trying to figure out what had gone wrong with Catherine?

"This is quite a man cave, isn't it?" I observed.

"The whole house is," Catherine said, picking up one of the heavy marble coasters from a walnut occasional table. "It's odd... I've spent so much time here, but it seems a lifetime ago."

"Funny, isn't it? Sometimes, when I get an e-mail from one of my Austin friends, it feels like only yesterday that I moved to the island... but at the same time, I feel like I've been here my whole life."

"Time is a strange thing," she said. "And old things keep cropping up this week." I knew she was thinking of Mandy —and the photo she had found under Brandon's bed.

My eyes flitted around the room, looking for anything of interest. On one of the end-tables I spotted a manila folder with a few pages sticking out from the corner. I reached for it and flipped it open; to my surprise, inside was a stack of articles about Brandon Marks.

I leafed through them; they were biographical pieces, mainly, about how he'd built his social media company WhatsIn from the ground up. At the mention of social media, I thought of Tania's dormant accounts, and wondered if Tania's disappearance might be linked to the arrival of Brandon. As far as I knew, the two weren't connected, and it was a long shot, but I couldn't rule anything out. I tucked the thought into the back of my mind, feeling uneasy about it, and read on.

One article in particular caught my interest; it covered Brandon's early life. "After spending much of his childhood in a small town in Maine, where the only way to the mainland was a mail boat that made the crossing a half dozen times a day, Marks moved to Silicon Valley after dropping out of college. He managed to leverage a clever idea into one of the biggest tech companies in the country." Next to the article was a photo of a young Brandon, squinting into the sun from the bow of a skiff. I grabbed my phone and pulled up the photo I had found in Brandon's room.

"Catherine, is it my imagination, or is this the same person?" I asked, hurrying over to show her the two pictures.

"I think it is," she said. "But I don't recognize his name."

I scanned the article. "Me neither."

"Oh," she said slowly, looking back and forth from the photo on my phone to the photo in the magazine. "I know who that is. That's Brendan Marksburg; he spent summers on the island when John was a kid. I didn't recognize him; I can't believe it's the same person!"

"He changed his name, then. I wonder why?" I mused.

"He was a different kid. So... withdrawn. Always walking the shores by himself, looking for wreckage with a metal detector; he was obsessed with shipwrecks. He didn't spend much time with the other kids; he used to always mess with old radios and things, and spent all his time trying to make them work."

"It seemed to have benefited him in the long run," I commented.

"Yes, but he was always a loner. Never had any friends."

"I'm not sure he does now, frankly. He's got people who work for him, but the relationships seem superficial. Employer-employee, but nothing more."

"He always did seem more interested in things than people," she said. As she spoke, Murray materialized from the bowels of the massive house, dressed nattily (for him) in green plaid golf pants and a spearmint-colored Polo shirt. He'd even taken the time to shave, and I caught a whiff of piney aftershave from across the room.

"Well," he said. "It's good to see you both. Can I get you ladies a drink?"

"Just a club soda, if you have it," Catherine said.

"Water, please," I said. He walked over to what appeared to be a built-in bookshelf and opened two doors to reveal a wet bar. Beneath it was a mini fridge, from which he retrieved a can of Canada Dry and some ice.

"Are you sure I can't get you something stronger?" he asked. "It's been quite a week."

"Just club soda. And yes, it has," Catherine agreed. "I found your handyman outside my carriage house this morning, Murray."

"I heard," Murray said as he popped the small glass bottle open and poured it over ice, then filled a second glass with tap water for me. "I can't figure out what he was doing in your neck of the woods," Murray said. "Did you hire him to do some work?" he asked me, walking over and handing Catherine her glass. Their eyes met briefly; she colored and looked away. He gazed at her, looking a little like a moonstruck calf, before retreating to the other wing chair. I noticed he leaned toward her, though, as if she had some sort of gravitational pull.

"No," I said. "I actually wondered why you kept him on; he seemed kind of nosy the one time I hired him. I found him going through my desk."

"Did you," he said, rather than asked, his eyes turning to me. The easiness was gone, somehow, and his beady eyes fixed on me as if I were prey... or a potential predator. "Did he find anything juicy? A hidden secret or two?"

"I don't really have any secrets," I said, finding it interesting that he should immediately leap to that conclusion, as opposed to thinking Steve might have been looking for credit card numbers or other financial information. "But other people might."

"No secrets here," he said in a jolly voice, but his eyes

darted to the painting above the fireplace. What was back there? I wondered. A safe behind the painting, maybe? With something he didn't want anyone else to know about?

"What kind of work did he do for you?" I asked.

"Oh, this and that," he said. "A place this big always needs painting, or siding replaced, or window frames fixed... you know how it is. It is a bit curious that he ended up at your place. A tiff with one of your guests, maybe? Although I hear they put the cuffs on Tom today."

"They did," I said. "But I don't believe he did it. We were wondering, since he spent so much time around here, whether you knew if he'd had issues with anyone else on the island."

"So you didn't just come to bring me cookies and visit," he said, eyeing the plate of sugar cookies.

"Oh... I forgot," she said, blushing and putting the plate on the table. "I know you had a working relationship that went back quite a ways; I'm sorry you lost him."

"It wasn't anything other than a working relationship, but I'll take the cookies," he said, eyeing the plate with interest. "Sugar cookies?"

"My mother's recipe," I said. "Go ahead."

"Don't mind if I do," he said, lifting the plastic wrap and pulling out a pale round. I could see the sugar glinting as he bit into it. A row of windows lined the back wall of the room, framing the large swimming pool he'd recently built behind the house (rarely used, from what Catherine told me) along with a sweeping view of the Gulf of Maine beyond. "Delicious," he mumbled through a mouthful of crumbs.

"Back to Steve, though," Catherine said. "What do you know about him?"

Murray finished off the cookie before answering. "He

kept to himself. Was a good worker. We never had any problems."

"You didn't find him nosy at all?" I asked.

"He kept to his work," Murray said coolly. "We didn't have any issues."

His eyes were roving around the room, now... I could tell he was uncomfortable with the line of conversation. "What jobs was he working on?" I asked, as Catherine sat primly nearby. There was a tension in the room that didn't just come from my line of questioning; I could tell she still had feelings for Murray, and not all of them were good.

"I didn't really keep track," Murray said, darting a longing glance at Catherine. "We kind of worked on a retainer system," he continued. "He was painting the front railings, as I recall."

"It's hard to keep up with all that wood, isn't it?" I asked.

"It is," he said. Then he cocked his round head to one side, as if just thinking of something. "Now that I think of it, he did mention a little bit of a dust-up with the Jamesons."

"He did work for them too, didn't he?"

"He did, until last summer; I think Jameson let him go."

"Why?"

Murray shrugged. "Ran out of money? Who knows? I don't keep track of my neighbors' finances."

I didn't believe that for a moment. Anyone as competitive as Murray kept track of all his neighbors' finances.

"I noticed you have some articles on Brandon Marks," Catherine said, pointing to the manila folder on the table.

"What?" He grabbed the file. "I have an assistant who clips articles for me," he said, shoving it under his arm and shrugging it off. "She sent this to me as a curiosity."

"Right," I said, not believing it for a moment.

"So what's behind the painting over the fireplace?" I asked Catherine as the massive front door of Murray's house closed behind us a few minutes later.

"What do you mean?" she asked, reaching up to pat her hair and glancing back behind her. I stole a backward glance, too; Murray was still standing at the window beside the door, eyes fixed on my lovely mother-in-law.

"Just a hunch," I said. "He kept looking at it when I talked about Steve prying into things. I wondered if there was a safe or something back there."

"I don't know," she said, "but I know he's got things stashed away."

"He still has feelings for you, you know."

"Does he?" she asked in a light tone that was completely unconvincing.

"He does. I never did find out why you two broke up." Not that I hadn't probed; she'd repeatedly dodged questions from both John and me.

"I think he was two-timing me," she admitted, her face flushing pink.

"You *think*?"

She nodded.

"You don't know for sure?"

"I just... he was hiding the fact that he was having dinner with another woman... what was I supposed to think?"

I tried not to roll my eyes. The two of them were acting like teenagers.

"You could talk to him, you know."

"I could," she said. "But... there are other things, too. You know how he is. I always felt like he was keeping something from me, somehow."

"You don't seem to be sure breaking up was the right thing to do," I said. "Have you really talked with him?"

"I've thought about reaching out to him, but I just don't know."

"You've got to follow your instinct," I said, "but I feel like there's unfinished business there."

"I thought you didn't like Murray?" she said, eyeing me sideways.

"We've never gotten along particularly well," I said. "But you two spent a lot of time together. It doesn't seem right to just let things go without at least discussing what went wrong. After all, you're living on the same island."

She pursed her lips. "For now, anyway."

"Wait. What?"

"I... I was thinking I might move back to Boston."

"No!" I was a bit taken aback by my own vehemence. When Catherine had moved to the island, I'd had some trepidation about how things were going—after all, we were very different people—but I'd come to love having her in the carriage house behind the inn. "Why?"

"I just... it's hard being here. I'd like to have an opportunity to find a partner, but here on the island, there aren't exactly a ton of prospects. Plus, every time I turn around, there's Murray."

"I can see that," I said, "but we love having you here... I'd be so sad to see you go! Maybe you should talk to him, at least clear the air between you."

"No," she said, chin up. "If he wants to talk, he can come to me."

"All right," I said as we got back into the van. I wasn't sure that was the best course of action, but it wasn't my life; it was hers.

11

When we got back to the inn, Adam was there, a fretful expression on his handsome face. He was wearing the thick sweatpants he favored for days out on the water, along with the red wool hat Gwen had knitted him for his birthday.

"What's wrong?" I asked.

"It's Gwen," he said. "She can't hold anything down; I have to struggle to get water into her. I've got to go out and haul traps, but I didn't want to leave her alone."

"Where is she?"

"Upstairs sleeping," he said. "If she's not better, I may take her to the emergency room tonight."

"Has she been to a doctor yet?"

"She keeps saying she'll go, but she hasn't yet. I think the boat ride makes her more nauseous."

"She's going to have to get over that unless we can find someone who still makes house calls."

"I know someone, actually," Catherine said. "She retired a couple of months ago, but she might be willing to come take a look at her. Let me call her and see if she can make it over."

"I'm going to go check on Gwen now," I said.

"I'm coming up with you," Adam told me. "Maybe together we can talk some sense into her."

"I'll let you know what Barbara says," Catherine said as she pulled up the contacts on her phone.

Adam followed me up the stairs to the room that used to be Gwen's. I knocked lightly.

"Come in," she answered in a scratchy, weak voice.

I stepped into the dark room; the curtains were drawn, and I could just make out her pale face against the darkness of her hair.

"You don't sound so good," I said.

"I'm okay," she said.

"No you're not," Adam corrected her. "You haven't eaten in three days, and you can barely hold down a teaspoon of water." He sat down on the edge of the bed and reached for her wrist, feeling for her pulse. "Your heart rate's way up," he informed her. "You're dangerously dehydrated. We need to take you in."

"I'll drink something," she said. "I promise. Just... I can't handle the mail boat right now."

"Will you try broth?" I asked. "The salt might help."

"I'll try," she said.

"I'll go heat some up. Adam, if you need to go, I've got her."

"The traps can wait," he announced. "I'm going to make sure she keeps this broth down, or I'm taking her in the skiff this afternoon."

"Adam..."

"Honey, I'm worried about you. The lobsters aren't going anywhere; they can wait."

"Are you sure?"

"Positive," he said in a tender voice, leaning over to kiss her forehead.

I headed for the stairs, turning at the doorway; Adam was gently stroking the hair from Gwen's forehead. She murmured something I couldn't make out as I closed the door behind me.

"Any luck?" I asked Catherine, who was sitting at the kitchen table with a glass of water.

"She's in Bangor today," she said, "but will make the trip tomorrow if we need her."

"Not ideal, but it's something," I said.

"How is she?"

"Dehydrated. Weak. I'm worried about her," I said as I pulled a container of broth from the freezer. "She hasn't eaten in three days and she's not keeping liquids down. If she can't keep down a cup of broth, Adam's going to take her to the mainland in his skiff this afternoon."

"I think that's a good call," Catherine said.

"I'm not sure she agrees with you, but I do," I told her as I ran hot water over the outside of the plastic container until I could loosen the block of frozen broth. I dumped it into a glass mug and popped it into the microwave, then sat down across from Catherine.

"I hope she'll be okay. Think it's flu?"

"If so, she's the only one on the island who's got it, at least that I know of. Whatever it is, I hope she clears it quickly."

"Me too." I hoped whatever was ailing Gwen would pass soon; I knew Adam would be by her side the whole time. I was still worried about Tania, too. I hadn't heard anything from Charlene, and I still didn't know if the police were chasing down the Instagram lead. The not-knowing was hard.

"I've been thinking about what you said about Murray," Catherine told me, staring at the ice in her glass. "You may be right. I've spent my whole life not saying what I think or asking for what I need. It may be time to practice some direct communication for a change."

"I'll be curious to see what he says," I told her.

"Me too." She looked up at me. "Should I call him?"

"You could," I said. "Tell him you'd like to talk."

"What if he doesn't want to?"

I shrugged. "Well, then, at least you tried."

She took a sip of water and set the glass down on the table. "I'll think about it," she said.

"Good," I told her. "Clarity helps." As I spoke, the microwave dinged. I removed the bowl of broth, putting it on a tray with a glass of water, a napkin and a spoon, and carried it upstairs.

"Hope she keeps it down," Catherine said. "Give her a kiss from me."

"I will," I promised.

Adam and Gwen were conversing in low tones as I walked in; he was holding her hand in his and looking at her intently. Biscuit and Smudge had both taken advantage of the opportunity for a daytime nap, and were tucked in next to her; Smudge purred loudly and looked up at me with half-closed eyes, the picture of feline contentment. As I set the tray down on the table by her bed, Adam turned and thanked me.

"My pleasure," I said, hoping Gwen would reach for the mug, but her eyes remained fixed on Adam. She gave him a slight nod as I turned back toward the door.

"You heard about Tom?" he asked as I was about to leave the room.

"I did," I said, pausing at the doorway and turning around. "Do you know anything about it?"

"I don't know anything about... the way Steve died, or how," he said, "but I do know that he was a jerk."

12

"What do you mean?" I asked. When he didn't answer, I said, "You know something, don't you? And you feel bad about telling me."

"It's just something I overheard," he said. "I don't like jumping to conclusions, or causing trouble where there doesn't need to be, but with Tom arrested..."

"Tell me," I said.

"You know how there's a trail behind my cottage?"

"I do," I said.

"Well, I was coming back from the co-op along the trail the day you found that young girl's remains next to the U-Boat. I was just about to get to the fork when I overheard some voices." He ran a hand through his thick mop of hair, and his mouth turned down into a frown. "I stopped—I don't know why, but there was something about the voices that made me not want them to know I was there." He paused, looking torn in the dim light.

Gwen squeezed his hand, and in a faint voice, said, "Go on, sweetheart."

"Right. Okay. Well... It was two men. One of them was

Steve... I'm almost sure of it. He always had that slight lisp on the s that's very recognizable. The other one I didn't recognize, but there was a bit of a Boston twang to it. At least I think so. Anyway... Steve said something about that night on the Barbary, and how now things were a little different. The other man, the one with a Boston accent, said it was ancient history and nobody would believe him anyway, and that there wasn't any proof. And then he called him a blood-sucking leech who had gotten enough already, and that he wasn't paying another dime. Steve said to the Boston guy that he had until the next morning to decide. The Boston guy started yelling, but then I shifted my weight to adjust my backpack and a stick broke under my boot, and it got quiet. I heard footsteps heading both directions, moving fast, like they didn't want to be seen or heard. I didn't run into either of them the rest of the way home."

"The Barbary," I said. "That sounds like it could be the name of a boat."

"I thought that, too, but I don't know of any vessel with that name around here," Adam said. "I guess I could go talk to the Harbor Master and see if there's any record of a Barbary."

I thought of Mandy's disappearance; Steve was on the island at the time it happened. It was kind of a wild connection to make, but was it possible that Steve knew what happened to Mandy and was blackmailing someone to stay quiet about it? Somebody had tied her to the killick and sunk her. I just hoped she was gone before they put her in the water, I thought with a shudder. "I'd start by checking the times around when Mandy disappeared."

"That was exactly my thought," Adam said solemnly. "The only 'ancient history' turning up the last few days is Mandy's remains. But I do know that whoever Steve was talking to, it wasn't Tom. If we can find out what that conversation was about, and who Steve was talking to, they might drop the charges against him."

"Unfortunately, I think we're going to have to come up with more than that," I said. "Apparently he dated Mandy way back when. The police are short-staffed, John told me, and they're thinking he might be involved in both deaths. It would be a quick resolution to both cases for them, so we're definitely going to need more than a conversation you overheard to convince them to look into it more."

"Like an actual suspect, and a concrete motive?" He grimaced.

"Like that," I said. "On the plus side, if you're right and there's blackmail involved, then that would certainly qualify, so at least we have a potential lead. If Steve did know what happened to Mandy, and the person responsible for her death was on the island when she disappeared and is still here now, then it narrows things down."

"It does," Gwen agreed in her faint voice. I thought again of the photo Catherine had found under Brandon's bed. Why had he had it? And was one of the people in it Mandy's killer?

I thought again of Brandon, who had spent summers on the island off to himself. Had he been responsible for what happened to her? He didn't exactly have a Boston accent, but it was definitely Northeastern. And he had been here when Mandy went missing.

But if he was responsible for killing a young woman and sinking her body, why hire a research vessel to scan the coast of Maine?

Maybe he wasn't the killer, I thought. Maybe he thought he knew what had happened and was looking for proof? No, I decided; that would be looking for a needle in a haystack.

Finding the body was a total fluke; it was one thing to look for a submarine, another to look for the remains of someone who disappeared twenty years ago.

Still, if he had killed Mandy all those years ago, wouldn't it make sense that he'd want nothing to do with scanning the ocean floor near where he'd disposed of a body?

There was something here I was missing, I decided.

I just wish I knew what.

"Aunt Nat?"

"What? Oh," I said, bringing my mind back to the dark room with my sick niece and her worried husband. "Sorry. Just woolgathering. Did you try the broth yet, by the way?"

She grimaced and propped herself up on the pillows. Adam picked up the mug of broth and raised it to her lips. She took a few sips, then held up a hand. "I can't do more. Let me see if I can keep that down."

"Do you want an audiobook to listen to, to distract you?" I suggested.

"Thanks, but it won't make a difference. I've tried everything... ginger ale, peppermint tea, Tums, Saltine crackers... nothing seems to work."

"We'll get you sorted out," Adam said. "I promise."

"Thanks, baby," she said in a quiet voice.

"I'll leave you two," I said, "but if Brandon turns up, I may call you so you can say hello to him. See if his was the voice you heard."

"If I can recognize it," he said. "Was he here on the island when Mandy disappeared?"

"He was, under another name," I said.

"How do you know?" Gwen asked, and I told her about our trip to Murray's.

"Weird," Gwen said. "Why change your name?"

"I have no idea, but I hope to find out," I said. It was on my list of things to Google.

"I hope Catherine talks to Murray," my niece fretted. "She's lonely. I can't stand Murray, but he did seem to make her happy."

"We'll see."

"Any word on Tania?" Gwen asked.

"Not yet, but we have some social media leads the detectives are checking out."

"She said something about big news the other day when I saw her at the store," Gwen said. "She was very secretive about it... said her Aunt Charlene would be just blown away."

"What kind of big news?"

"I don't know, but she was awfully excited. Said her aunt would be super proud of her."

"Do you have her number?"

"I do," Gwen confirmed.

"Have you tried texting her?"

"No, but I will. Are you thinking maybe she'd be more likely to respond to someone who wasn't Charlene?"

"Exactly," I said. "Now drink that broth, Missy. I'll let you get some rest."

"Thanks," she said. "And don't worry; I'm sure it's just a stomach bug."

"You've had it for a month," Adam said. "That's a little long for a stomach bug."

"Oh, it's fine. I gained a little weight last winter anyway; maybe this is just my body's way of shedding it."

If Gwen had gained weight, I was a pink narwhal, but I kept my mouth shut; my niece had never been anything but slender, but there was no point in contradicting her. "Keep me posted," I told them, and then headed down to the kitchen.

Catherine was gone, and there wasn't much else I could do right now, so I pulled a canister of flour out of the cabinet and flipped through my recipe binder until I found something I had the ingredients for. I settled on a fudgy Bundt cake—it would use up the last of the cocoa and sour cream I'd brought back from the mainland last week—and set to work assembling it.

Once I gathered the ingredients together for the cake, I flipped open my laptop and typed in Brandon's name.

A number of articles came up, including a few of the ones I'd seen in Murray's manila folder. Brilliant but reclusive entrepreneur with all kinds of interests and plans. Made his fortune early, and now spent his time hunting down shipwrecks and trying to design a self-driving car.

As I warmed leftover coffee, butter, and cocoa on the stove, I scanned article after article, but most of them focused on his business career. I wanted to know about what came earlier—how he ended up on the island, whether he still had any personal connections, and why he'd changed his name. When the butter was melted, I whisked the contents of the pot and put them aside to cool, then typed in Brendan Marksburg and hit SEARCH.

The third entry that came up was a hit; it came from the *Daily Mail*. It was dated July, one year before Mandy disappeared.

SUMMER VISITOR SUSPECTED OF ARSON.

No wonder Brandon changed his name, I thought as I began reading. Apparently Brendan had been identified as potentially responsible for the burning of three empty buildings, two on Cranberry Island and one in Northeast Harbor, in the space of six weeks. He told the police he was "interested in observing the way and rate at which fire spread," but did not admit to setting the fires. I couldn't tell if he had been convicted, but further research showed that he changed his name two years later, at twenty. It was a good thing for him his dalliance with fire had occurred before the digital age, I thought, or there would be no escaping the ashes of his past, so to speak, but he seemed somehow to have pulled it off.

I thought about the conversation Adam had overheard as I whisked the dry ingredients into a bowl, then added the cooled chocolate mixture. Was Steve threatening to blackmail Brendan over his history of arson, and not the murder of Mandy? It was possible. I Googled "arson" and "Marksburg" and discovered that he hadn't been convicted because of a lack of evidence.

Still, I reflected as I whisked eggs into a mixture of sour cream and vanilla, then incorporated it into the chocolatey batter. How had this not turned up in any of the articles written about him? I was sure it wasn't something he wanted in the news.

John walked in as I had finished pouring the batter into my Bundt pan and was about to slide it into the oven. Once the cake had baked and cooled, I'd make the frosting—a decadent mix of chocolate and cream—and drizzle it over the top.

"Hey, you," he said, coming up and giving me a quick kiss. "What just went into the oven? It looks like it's going to be amazing."

"Fudge Bundt cake," I answered, then brought him up to date on Gwen.

"The cake sounds amazing, but I don't like what's going on with Gwen," he said. "I'm glad Adam's staying with her; it sounds like she needs to be looked at, though."

"Any word on Tania?" I asked.

"They found where that Instagram photo was taken," he said.

"Really? Are they going out to find her?"

"It was right near the University of Maine campus in Orono," he said. "Do you know if she has any friends there?"

"Not that I know of, but Charlene might know more than I do," I said. "Anything else turn up?"

"Afraid not," he said. "She's not been posting anything since then."

"Shoot," I said. "On the plus side, at least we know she's recently been near a university, and not out at some deserted camp by a lake in the middle of the Maine woods."

"I guess there's that," he said, "but I'd still be happier knowing where she is."

"You and me and Charlene," I said. I grabbed my phone and called my friend, but she didn't pick up. I left her a message relaying what John had told me and told her to call me.

"Who's here for dinner tonight?" John asked when I hung up.

"Unless I hear otherwise from Rebecca, I think it's just us, along with Max and Ellie."

"I've enjoyed meeting them," he said. "I hope their stay hasn't been ruined by everything that happens."

"Everyone else's week has," I said. "And Max was helpful with the social media thing tracking down Tania. She's got two teenaged daughters of her own, so she's got some insight."

There was a long silence. John leaned up against the wall near me and studied my face as I cleaned up a bit of stray flour from the counter. "Do you regret not having children?" he asked suddenly.

I put down the sponge I was using. "Whoa," I said. "Where did that come from?"

"I was just thinking about how Gwen is like a daughter to you, but you never had the chance to have a daughter of your own. Do you regret it? Do you still want one?"

I thought about the question for a moment. I had wanted children for a while, in my early thirties, but at the time I was not at all with the right man. And by the time I found the right man, I was so wrapped up with my life at the inn and on the island and Gwen that those longings had been subsumed by other projects.

Were they still there? I took a deep breath and closed my eyes, searching my feelings.

"I don't know," I said truthfully after a long pause. "I love my life the way it is. Gwen is like a daughter to me, and you and I are so busy with the inn and our other pursuits it would be hard to have the time to devote to a child." I looked at him, studying his green eyes. "Do you want one?"

"I thought so, for a while," he said. "But now... I just don't know. I really love the life we've created, and I don't want to upset the balance we've achieved. Plus, you're right; don't tell your sister, but Gwen really is like a daughter to me."

"It's probably too late for me to have a kid anyway," I said, "so this conversation is most likely academic."

"I'm sure we could if we wanted to," John reassured me. "But we really have to want to. It's a big decision."

"Do you want kids?" I asked again.

"I am honestly fine either way," he told me, and I could see by the steadiness of his eyes that he was telling me the truth. "But I want to be sure you make the decision that's right for you."

"I'll think about it," I said. "Thank you so much for asking, though."

"Of course," he said. "Always."

He pulled me into a big, woodsy-smelling hug, and I felt myself relax as I pressed the side of my face into his flannel-clad chest. Hugging him always made me feel safe.

As he released me, I heard footsteps on the stairs; it was Adam.

"Did Gwen manage to drink the broth?" I asked.

"Half of it," he said. "And it hasn't come back up yet; she fell asleep, or I would have made her drink more. Should we take her over to the mainland tonight, do you think?"

"Let's let her sleep a bit and see if we can get her to drink some more," I suggested. "Did you take her pulse again?"

"It's a little better, but it's still high."

"Catherine's friend said she can do a house call tomorrow, which means Gwen could skip the boat ride." I turned to John. "What do you think?"

"If she can drink and keep it down tonight, maybe," he said, "but I'm concerned. She's got a lot of ground to make up."

"I'll make sure she does it," Adam promised, then returned up the stairs to Gwen's bedside.

"He really does love her," I said after he'd disappeared.

"He does. And I love you," John said, kissing the top of my head, then giving me a sly grin. "And I might love you even more if you let me have some of that cake when it comes out of the oven. It smells amazing."

"I will," I promised, "as long as you help me get dinner together."

"What are we having?"

"Chicken pot pie," I said, "with leftover roast chicken from the other day. I froze some pie crust a few weeks ago, but I'll need a sous chef to chop veggies."

"I'm your man," he said. "And those gluten-free folks have no idea what they're missing."

I laughed. "Thanks for reminding me; I have a recipe for dairy-free pumpkin custard I meant to make. Of course, I have no idea if or when they'll be here to eat it, but I thought it would be good to have in the fridge just in case."

"Sounds good to me," he said, "and just right for this fall weather. The sky is a perfect blue, and I think the maples are at their peak."

"They are, aren't they?" I said, glancing out the window at the brilliant red maples against the dark green backdrop of tall spruces and pines.

I just wished Tania were here on the island to see them.

13

Dinner was a cozy affair. I took some pot pie up to Adam; Gwen had finally managed to keep down not just one, but two cups of broth, and her heart rate had dropped enough that it seemed safe to wait for tomorrow's house call.

"Has it been this bad before?" I asked him as Gwen dozed off.

"She hasn't been well for a few weeks, but it's the first time it's been this bad," he said. "I'm worried."

"We'll make sure she's taken care of," I told him. "Do you want to come down and join us for dinner?"

"I'd rather stay here with her, to be honest," he said. "I brought a copy of *Two Years Before the Mast*."

"I'll bring some up for you," I promised. "And if you need another book, you're welcome to pick one from the library downstairs."

"Thanks!"

As John chopped vegetables, I told him what Adam had passed on to me upstairs.

Max and Ellie invited John and me to join them, so we

had a very companionable meal in the dining room. The temperature dropped as the sun did, so the warm, rich pot pie, studded with carrots and celery and my secret ingredient, leeks, was perfect with a glass of Pinot Gris Max had picked up on the mainland and kindly shared with us. I had paired the pot pie with salad for a bit of greenery; dessert was warm fudge cake, along with a little of my secret stash of Blue Bell Homemade Vanilla ice cream, accompanied by coffee.

"University of Maine," Max said when we reported what the police had found out about Tania's Instagram post. "Not exactly a romantic B&B, is it? Kind of an odd place for a romantic assignation, unless whoever she's with is a student."

"That's what I thought, too," I said.

"They've sent a picture and are alerting the local police," John said. "With luck, she'll turn up soon."

"Unlike that poor girl who disappeared all those years ago," Ellie said. "I heard someone say they arrested someone local."

"They did," I said, "but I'm not convinced they've got the right person." I looked at John; I'd told him what I'd learned from Adam earlier while we were making dinner.

"Boston accent. Interesting," he said.

"Are there a lot of people from Boston on the island?" Max asked.

"Quite a few, actually," I said. "Particularly in summer."

"My family did the same thing, only in Snug Harbor," she said. "I spent summers there as a kid; it's still one of my favorite places in the world."

"I do love Snug Harbor," I said. "It's such a cute town, and it's got lots of potential for a store! If I hadn't moved to Cranberry Island, I might consider starting an inn there;

the coastline is gorgeous, and there are so many neat shops!"

"And tons of gorgeous places to hike," she said, her eyes lighting up for the first time since I'd met her. "I'd love to live there, and have something like you have here."

"You've been in the book business a long time, it seems," I said.

"Oh, yes," she said. " I used to help Loretta out with stocking the shelves and running the registers part-time when I got older." She glanced at Ellie. "So I guess I got my start early."

"You're a natural," Ellie said.

"Thanks," Max said, blushing a little bit. "Whether Loretta wants to give the shop up or not, I think I'll offer to help her clean it up; it's in disrepair, or at least it was when I was there last year. I didn't say anything, but the place just hasn't been kept up like it used to be. It was kind of sad, actually."

"I think you should get in touch with her," Ellie reiterated. "Even if she doesn't want to give up the shop, she might appreciate it if you offered to partner with her, and bring the place back to life. And you could stay at your mom's camp, at least until you found a better place; real estate prices are better in Snug Harbor than Boston.".

"I never thought I'd say it," John said, "but I love having my mother next door, actually."

"I'm not so sure that would work for us," Max said. "Our relationship has been... well, let's call it tempestuous. But it might be a good call for the short term."

"Don't rule anything out at this stage," I advised. "You never know what will happen!" As I speared a carrot from my pot pie, the phone rang. I excused myself to pick up; it was Charlene.

"Thanks for calling earlier; my phone's been wonky. Terrible timing; what if Tania tried to reach me and I couldn't answer?"

I resisted the urge to ask if she'd heard anything; if she had, she would have told me. "I'm sure she'd leave a message," I told her.

"What a terrible week this has been," she moaned.

"Do you want to come over?" I asked. "I've got leftover pot pie and fudge cake."

"I'm not really hungry, but I could use company tonight... do you mind?" she asked.

"Of course not! Come on over!" I said. "You're welcome to stay the night, too."

"I'll head out in a few. Thanks, Nat," she told me. "You're the best friend ever."

I hung up and returned to the dining room, where there was a lively discussion of whale watching expeditions in Snug Harbor.

"Charlene's on her way," I told them.

"How's she doing?" Max asked.

"Stressed," I said. "Worried sick."

"Of course she is," Max murmured. "Poor thing. Particularly since they found that missing girl from twenty years ago."

"They sure made that arrest fast."

"They did," John confirmed, his mouth tugging down at the corner.

"You don't think they got the right person, though," Max observed. "Why?"

"I've known Tom almost my whole life," John said. "I think they may have made a mistake."

"That's rough," Max said.

As she spoke, the front door opened. A moment later,

Brandon and his entourage appeared at the door to the dining room.

"We're back for dinner," Rebecca announced.

"You were supposed to let me know by four if you were eating here," I said.

"It's been a busy day," she said.

I sighed. "Give me twenty minutes and I'll see what I can do."

John raised an eyebrow. I shook my head slightly; I'd bill them handsomely, I'd decided.

As I stood up, John did, too. "No... stay here," I told him. "I've got an idea of what I'll do; you can clean up. Besides, someone needs to keep Charlene company when she gets here."

"If you change your mind..." he said.

"I'll come find you," I promised.

I retreated to the kitchen, already formulating a plan. I had several options on hand intended to meet their dietary requirements, including coconut milk, vegetables, and a container of firm tofu. I scooped rice into the rice cooker, added water, and set it to cook, then grabbed the ingredients for a Thai curry from the fridge.

As I finished slicing the tofu and set it on a paper towel to drain, Charlene appeared at the door. Not for the first time, I wished my cousin Robert lived on Cranberry Island, not Bangor. They'd been dating long-distance for a while. It was too bad he was in Australia right now; Charlene was having to make do with phone calls when he had a break between sessions. I knew he wanted nothing more than to be by her side, but the timing was awful.

"Hi," I said, giving her a hug. She smelled of fall leaves and crisp salt air, but her face was still drawn.

"Thanks for having me over," she said.

"I love having you here," I told her, giving her another squeeze. "I have to put together an impromptu dinner for some impolite guests, but John is in the dining room with Max and Ellie; they know you're coming."

"Impromptu dinner... the multimillionaire?"

"Yup. You know him, you know."

"Do I?"

"Remember Brendan Marksburg?" I asked.

"Wait... what?" She blinked. "That's him? The kid who set all those fires?"

"He changed his name, I guess to leave his past behind him."

"That's crazy! And now he owns like half the world."

"I know. I want to hear everything you can remember about him," I told her.

"Why?" Then her eyebrows rose. "You think he might have had something to do with what happened to Mandy?"

"I don't know, but he was on the island when Steve died, and on the island when Mandy died, too. It's kind of a weird coincidence, don't you think?"

"It is," she said. "I'll think about it... he was an odd duck."

"He's not exactly run-of-the-mill now, either," I informed her. "Pot pie is in the oven... help yourself. I'll be in as soon as I can.."

"How is our lovely Gwen?" Charlene asked as she pulled a plate from the cabinet.

"She's upstairs with Adam," I told her. "She kept two cups of broth down, so we're not making her go to the emergency room on the mainland tonight."

Charlene scooped a small portion of pot pie onto her plate, then returned the casserole to the oven. "What's going on with her, anyway?"

"She's just having a hard time keeping things down, and she's so thin that she can't really afford not to eat."

"I know," Charlene said. "She's always been a waif."

My niece was verging on skeletal now, I thought as I chopped up an onion and then reached for a bell pepper. "She's been under so much stress this summer with the Art Guild, I'm wondering if that's not causing the trouble."

"She needs to get that checked out."

"We'll make sure she does," I reassured her.

"Could she be pregnant?" Charlene asked.

"I don't think so," I said. "She said they were waiting for the Art Guild to get better established before thinking about having a family."

"Well, things happen sometimes."

"That's true," I mused. It would be better than some awful condition, but I wasn't sure they were ready to start a new family yet. And I didn't know how to bring it up; I guessed I'd figure it out with time. "Ah, well. I'll find a way to ask her about it. Now go be social while I get this curry together."

"You need help?"

"I'm good," I said.

I finished chopping the veggies, poured some oil into a pan and let it heat. Once it was shimmering, I tossed in the tofu, letting it turn golden brown before turning it out onto a paper-towel lined plate. Then I added the veggies, sautéing them until they were slightly softened, before adding some of the curry paste I kept on hand and a can of coconut milk. While the curry cooked, I tossed together a quick salad, then drizzled it with some of the Asian dressing I had made a few days earlier; it was a delicious mix of rice wine vinegar, sesame oil, garlic, ginger, and a touch of soy, and would be perfect with the curry. When the veggies were cooked and the rice was done, I added the tofu back in. I plated four salads and took them out to the dining room; Ellie, Max and John were busy keeping Charlene distracted. I headed up the stairs to tell Brandon and his entourage that dinner was ready.

I was about to knock on his door when I realized it was ajar. Someone was talking inside.

"You never told me you spent time here." It was a woman's voice; it must be Rebecca.

"It wasn't relevant." Brandon's voice was unmistakable. It did have a bit of Boston in it, and I recalled reading that he'd attended Harvard before dropping out. Could he be the mystery speaker?

"That man asked if you'd burned down any buildings lately. What the heck is that all about?"

"Childhood experiments," he said. "And please stop asking questions."

"Did you know the guy who died, too?" she asked.

"Again," Brandon said in a flat voice. "Please stop asking questions. I hired you to be my assistant, not my interrogator."

That seemed to work, since she didn't respond.

I padded backward down the hall a few steps, then walked back to the door and knocked. "Dinner's ready downstairs," I announced when Rebecca opened the door a few inches. Behind her stood Brandon, his back to the door, staring out at the water, as usual.

"Thank you," she said politely, but distractedly. There was a small groove between her brows I hadn't seen before; she looked worried. "We'll be down shortly."

I retreated back downstairs, my curiosity about Brandon inflamed even more. Had he been responsible for what had happened to Mandy all those years ago? And had he killed again, here on the island?

If so, why?

Was it because Steve knew he was a killer?

Again, it didn't make sense; why comb the bottom of the ocean if you knew you'd left a body there?

I was missing something. I just didn't know what.

"Hey," I said quietly to Charlene and John as I walked back through the dining room. "Do either of you know if Brandon had anything to do with Mandy way back when?"

"He had a crush on her," Charlene told me. "He sent her a long poem once, in meter. She thought it was funny."

I winced at the cruelty of youth.

"Did she tell him that?" I asked.

"Oh, yes," Charlene said. "It was horrible."

I caught John's eye, and I could tell he and I were thinking the same thing.

Maybe we'd been harboring a murderer under our roof.

14

The curry was, if not glowingly received, at least not rejected, and nobody said thank you for the trouble, but since Brandon was not the most appreciative guest, I didn't take it personally. I just mentally added another twenty percent to his bill.

I had a bit of the curry myself; it was delicious, or at least I thought so, and I looked forward to enjoying some tomorrow for lunch. Once I'd finished wrapping up the leftovers, I cut myself a big slice of moist fudge cake and went into the dining room to join John and Charlene, who were still in conversation with Max and Ellie at the table.

"Did they go back upstairs?" I asked, referring to Brandon, Rebecca and Antoine.

"About ten minutes ago," John informed me.

I glanced at the doorway to the parlor. "Do you mind moving to the kitchen? I want to ask questions, but I don't want to risk being overheard."

"Got it," Max said.

"I'll put on a pot of coffee."

"Decaf, please," Charlene said. "I'm having a hard enough time sleeping as it is."

"I can add a shot of rum to it too if you like," I offered. "Or whiskey."

"Oooh, Irish Coffee sounds fabulous," Charlene said.

"I'll make you one," I offered.

"Can you make two?" Max asked.

"Or three?" John added.

"Irish coffee all around," I promised. "Let's go."

They all followed me into the buttery yellow kitchen, sitting down at my big farm table.

"I'll make coffee," John offered. As he ground beans and filled the filter, I retrieved cream from the fridge and reached for the whiskey I kept in a cabinet next to the laundry room.

"So, did you all remember anything else?" I asked as I assembled cups on the counter.

"Just that Brandon—Brendan—was desperately in love with Mandy," Charlene said. "He never talked to her, though. He never really talked to any of us. He just walked around the island, picking things up off the beach, and spent time assembling things in a shed at the house his parents rented."

"How long before Mandy disappeared did he send the poem?"

"It was at the beginning of the summer," John said, "if I remember correctly. He'd evidently been thinking about her all year. I can't imagine how long it took him to craft that poem, much less gather the courage to give it to her."

"It was cruel what she did," Charlene said.

"What did she do?" I asked.

"When we were all together, hanging out at the playground by the school and smoking cigarettes Tom had snuck from his parents' house, she sat on one of the swings and read the whole poem to all of us."

"Was Brandon there?" I asked.

"No," she said, "but he found out about it. Anytime anyone saw him that whole summer, they asked how his Wonder Witch was doing."

"Wonder Witch?"

"The name of the poem was 'The Wonder Witch is You.'"

"Ouch," I said.

"Kids are cruel," Charlene said, grimacing. "I still regret it."

"Me too," John admitted, wincing a little.

"And when did Mandy disappear?" I asked.

"It wasn't long after that," John said. "Maybe a few weeks." His expression was grim. "Maybe he was angry enough that he got rid of her? There isn't much to go on, is there?"

"Was there anyone else in her life?" I asked as I poured whiskey into each of the glasses.

"She was always interested in hooking up with one of the rich summer boys," Charlene said. "She was kind of obsessed with the idea of a wealthy Prince Charming coming and sweeping her into a life of luxury. Her parents were teachers, so they couldn't afford to rent a house on the island."

"The local rich boys didn't seem too interested in fulfilling the fantasy, alas," John said. "There were a couple of them here, but they largely kept to themselves. They all had access to their family's boats, so they spent a lot of time over on Mount Desert Island, trying to sneak into the bars on Bar Harbor. They didn't hang out with us."

"I remember the time one of them showed off his father's yacht to her," Charlene said. "She was sure he was going to ask her out on it, but he never did. She went on and on about him for weeks."

"Who was that?" I asked, pouring coffee and sugar into the glasses.

"One of the Jameson boys. He and the Karstadt kids hung out with each other, but not us."

"Is he still on the island?" I asked.

"He is, but only occasionally," she said. "Ed Jameson inherited the family's house, but he doesn't come up much, and when he does, he doesn't really mix with the locals. The Karstadts haven't been here for a few years, but they still maintain the house."

"Ed's been here on and off this summer," John said. "I've seen his yacht out a few times."

"He doesn't come to the store; he sends someone," Charlene said, "and one of his personal staff gets groceries from the mainland."

"Friendly," I said dryly, topping the coffees off with cream and shuttling them to the table.

"Oh, yes," she said. "He's a real treat. Murray tried to get close to him—rub shoulders, you know—but Jameson never wanted anything to do with him." She took a sip of coffee. "Oooh. This is marvelous."

"It is," Max agreed, taking a sip of her own. "I never think to make these. Why not?"

"They're better shared with friends," I said, taking a sip of my own coffee, enjoying the burn of the whiskey, the richness of the coffee, and the cool sweetness of the cream. I looked up at Charlene, who was licking cream off of her upper lip. "Murray was here in the summers, too, wasn't he?"

"Oh, he was," Charlene said, "but his dad put him to work in one of his offices early, so he didn't have a lot of chance to mingle. He only got a few weekends here; he spent the rest of the time down in Boston with his father."

"He does have a Boston accent, doesn't he?" I mused. "Was he on the island when Mandy died?"

"I really don't remember," Charlene said. "You're not thinking Murray might have done it?"

"Steve did work for him," I said. "And when Catherine and I were over there, he was acting a little squirrelly."

"Maybe I'm glad they broke up after all," John said.

"I don't think she's over him yet."

"If he ends up in jail for murder, that might help," he said.

"You think?"

"I don't know, but it's worth looking into," he said.

"We don't really have anything to look into with Mandy," I said, "but Steve has lived here for years. Think there might be some clue at his house?"

"The police have been over it, and they didn't find anything," John said.

"They're understaffed," I pointed out.

"You really plan on breaking and entering?" John said.

"I didn't say that," I said, not admitting that that was exactly what I was thinking.

"Don't do it, Nat," John said.

"Oh, all right," I said. "But somebody's got to figure out what happened to Steve, or Tom Lockhart is going to go away for a very long time."

∼

AFTER WE FINISHED our Irish coffees, Max and Ellie headed up to bed. As John cleaned up the kitchen, I padded up the stairs to Gwen's old room, knocking lightly.

"Come in," Adam said in a low voice.

Gwen was sleeping, an empty mug on the table next to her, and Adam sat on a chair next to the bed, his book open in his lap.

"How's she doing?" I whispered.

"Pulse rate is better and she kept it all down," he said, closing the book. "She even had a few bites of pot pie."

"Really? That's terrific!"

"I still want the doctor to come see her tomorrow, though," he said. "This has been going on for too long. I think she might have given herself an ulcer this summer."

"I've thought that, too," I said, speaking in a whisper. "We'll see what the doctor says. Are you staying here tonight?"

"Do you mind if I do?" he asked.

"Of course not," I said. "I've got a cot downstairs; want me to bring it up?"

"That would be great," he said. Gwen's bed was a single, and neither of us wanted to disturb her. "Hey..." I asked before I headed for the door. "Was it possible that the man with the Boston accent was Murray?"

He cocked his head. "It could be," he said. "I just don't know. Why?"

"Just a thought," I said. "I'll be right back with the cot."

"Thanks, Nat," he said.

I ran downstairs and retrieved the cot from the storage closet under the stairs. John took it up to Gwen's room for me, and Adam and I put on fresh sheets. "I'm going to head back down, but let me know if you need anything," I told him.

"Will do. And thanks again."

"Oh, anytime," I said. "Besides, you're family now."

"What an honor," he said, giving me a grateful smile before I nipped back down to the kitchen.

I made two more Irish coffees while John finished drying the pan I'd cooked the curry in. He had just sat down to join me when the phone rang.

I answered it; before I had the chance to say, "Gray Whale Inn," Lorraine's voice burst through the speaker.

"Nat, is that you? I have something to show you."

"What?" I asked.

"Just... Just come. And don't bring John, okay?"

"Why not?"

"Just don't. Please. For me."

She hung up before I could say anything else. I stood holding the phone in my hand, staring at John.

"What is it?" he asked.

"Lorraine has something to show me. But I'm supposed to go alone."

15

"I'm not sending you alone," John said.

"What. You think Lorraine's a murderer?" I asked.

"I have no idea who the murderer is," he said, "but I do know when someone asks you to come alone, you make sure you have back-up."

I sighed. "Well, what do I do?"

"I'm going with you," he said flatly.

"I'll tell you what. Why don't you wait in the van?"

"I still don't like it."

"I'm going. But if she's got something to tell me, I'm not going to hear it if you're there."

He sighed. "Okay. I'll compromise. You call me just before you go in there. Leave it on speaker, and I'll mute my phone. That way I'll be outside listening if anything goes wrong."

And presuming the phone actually worked, I thought but didn't say; phone service on the island was notoriously spotty.

"That works for me," I said. "We'll have those coffees when we get back," I said. "Or I'll make more."

"I'm glad she called when she did, or we wouldn't be able to drive."

"Even so, I'm going to have you drive," I said. "I feel a tad tipsy."

"I'm on it," he said.

It was a short drive to Lorraine's house. The upstairs windows were dark, but the lights downstairs were blazing when John pulled up.

I dialed him, then put the phone in my pocket as he picked up and muted his phone. "Ready?" I asked.

"Be careful," he said.

"Of course." I gave him a quick kiss on the cheek and opened the van door, curious what Lorraine wanted to show me.

I'd only knocked once before she flung the door open. "Oh, I'm so glad you came," she said, looking wild-eyed; there was a desperation to her voice that made me uncomfortable. "I found something today that I think might explain what happened to Steve Batterly."

"What is it?" I asked.

"I snuck into his house this afternoon to see what I could find."

"You're not supposed to do that!" I said, to some extent for John's benefit. He was always giving me a hard time about doing just that.

"I know, but I feel so... helpless. Tom is in jail and I can't just sit here doing nothing. Anyway, I found something the police missed."

"What? Where?"

"There was a loose floorboard in the bedroom; I noticed

it because it was a little bit off-kilter; it moved when I stepped on it. I pulled it up, and this is what I found." She pointed to a fat envelope on the table.

"I hate to ask this, but did you wear gloves?"

"I did," she said. "I've watched enough CSI to know the drill. I grabbed the rubber gloves from under the sink. I've got them right here." She produced a pair of yellow gloves and laid them on the table.

"What's in the envelope?"

"Take a look," she said.

I put on the gloves and opened the envelope. Inside was cash; a lot of cash. There were two stacks of hundreds and two stacks of fifties.

"That's a lot of money," I said. "Was there anything else?"

"Just a note," she said. "It's in the back, here. That's what I wanted you to see."

Inside was a handwritten chart of sorts. There were three columns, each headed by a letter— L, M, and E— and to the left was a line of dates; the timing went back about five years. L and M had numbers for multiple dates, between one and two thousand each time, about once a month. The third letter, E, had bigger amounts, about 5,000 each time, but had gone dormant a few years ago. There was a fourth column added on later, in pencil and then erased, with the letter T at the top.

"There's got to be fifty-thousand dollars here," I said, doing the math in my head.

"None of this money came from us," Lorraine said. "I'd know if it did; I do all the finances."

"Are you thinking this 'T' stood for Tom?"

"If so, you can tell right here he didn't get any money from him." There was desperation in her voice. "So there was no reason for Tom to hurt him."

Unless Tom had killed him before caving into blackmail demands, I thought but didn't say.

Lorraine continued, her voice fast and high. "He was getting this money from somewhere. I'm thinking maybe someone got tired of paying him, or if he was in some kind of drug dealing thing, something that went wrong somehow. Maybe somebody whose name started with M."

Murray? I wondered.

"You need to put this back where you found it," I advised her.

"If I do that, though, how am I going to tell the police I know what's there?"

"I'll... I'll convince John to take a look at the house, maybe," I said, wondering how John was taking all of this as he sat in the van outside.

"So I'm supposed to just put this back where I found it?"

"Yes," I said. "And don't go poking around anymore, okay?"

"But what about Tom?" she asked.

"We'll figure that out," I said. "For now, though, can you just put it back?"

"I will," she said. "As soon as the kids go to school tomorrow, I'll head back over."

"Good," I said. "And don't worry... I'm doing some investigating. I haven't given up on Tom."

"Really?" she asked. "I am so thankful. I just can't imagine the kids and me living without him."

"I know," I said. "I'm doing everything I can. Can I take a quick picture of this?"

"Okay," she said, "but are you sure that's a good idea? I'm not supposed to have it."

"You're right," I said. "Good thinking." I stared at it one more time, trying to commit it to memory.

"Thanks, Nat," she said. "I can't tell you how grateful I am."

I left a few minutes later, wondering what John would make of it all.

"You really scolded her for snooping?" he asked as I closed the van door behind me and he started the car.

"I did that for your benefit," I admitted, then told him what I'd seen.

"It sounds like a payoff record," he said.

"It does. And there was a ton of cash in there."

"Who was paying him off?"

"I'm guessing he was blackmailing people," I said. "And that Tom refused to play along; that's why he erased the T column."

"But who are M, E and L?"

"I'm guessing the M stands for Murray," I said, "but I don't know about the other two."

"I'll have to ask around and see who he was working for," John said. "I know he was snooping around the inn. I'm guessing he may have used his access to other people's house to dig up dirt, then hold their feet to the fire."

"Murray seemed wary when we were there and asking about Steve," I said as John turned toward the inn, the headlights illuminating the dark green pines lining the road. Cranberry Island usually seemed sweet and idyllic, but it was a moonless evening, and tonight it felt... sinister, somehow. "He kept glancing at the picture above the fireplace; I think he might have something hidden in a safe behind it."

"Unfortunately, there's no way to find that out without a warrant."

"If we 'find' the money with the list in Steve's house, would that be enough to get a warrant?"

"Maybe," he said, "but M is kind of nondescript. It might

be hard to convince a judge." And it could stand for Marksburg as easily as Murray.

"Did my mother ever talk to him, by the way?"

"I haven't seen her all day," I said. "I was so distracted with Gwen and everything else, I didn't even think about it."

"I'm going to check the carriage house the moment we get back to the inn," he said. "If Murray is a murderer, and she went to talk to him and let something slip..."

I felt a cold trickle of ice down my spine. "What would she let slip?"

"I don't know, but I don't want to risk my mother."

He hit the accelerator, and we made it home in record time. John practically hurled himself from the driver's seat and ran down the hill to the carriage house, which was dark. He pounded on the door, but from what I could see, there was no answer.

I hopped out of the van and hurried to the inn. The kitchen was empty; I hung my jacket on a peg and hurried into the dining room. It was also empty.

"Nat?"

It was Catherine's voice; she was sitting on the sofa in the living room, across from Charlene, who was stretched out on a chair by the fireplace, two Irish Coffee mugs on the table beside her.

"Oh, thank goodness," I breathed. "I'll let John know you're here."

"What? Why?"

"Hang on," I said, hurrying to the back door and pulling it open.

"She's here!" I called.

John whipped around, and I saw his shoulders sag in relief. "Where?"

"In the parlor," I said. "She's fine."

"Thank God," he said in a shaky voice, then loped up to the inn. I closed the door behind him, and together we headed back to the parlor.

"What did you think was wrong?" Catherine asked, looking confused, as John sat next to her on the couch and gave her a little hug.

"I don't know who the killer on the island is, and when you said you were going to talk to Murray and didn't come back..." He gave a sheepish shrug. "I guess I just let my imagination run away with me."

"I didn't talk with Murray, for your information," she said tartly. "I went for a long walk to clear my head. I still haven't come to a decision."

"Ah," I said. "I understand that. It's good to take some time."

"Why do you think he's a killer?"

John and I exchanged glances. I decided to let him share what he was comfortable with. "I think Steve may have been blackmailing some of the folks on the island. It's just a theory, of course."

"That makes sense," Catherine said, eyes widening. "I never did understand why Murray kept him on. In spite of what Murray may have told you, he was a terrible worker, and he was very... insolent. Murray always tolerated it, and I could never understand why."

"Do you have any idea what kind of information he might have had on Murray?"

"That's the thing... I have no idea. He's not married and he's no longer dating me," she said, "so it's probably not an affair, and he'd wound down his business dealings the last few years... I don't know what in the world Steve could have had on Murray."

"An illegal deal?" I suggested. "We both know he's not the most rule-bound person on the planet. Maybe he used to be mixed up in some stuff that wasn't completely aboveboard, and Steve found out about it?" I suggested.

Catherine pursed her lips. "It's possible, but I just don't know."

"Whatever it is, I'll bet he's got it hidden in his mansion somewhere," I said.

"The problem is, there's no way to find out," John pointed out. "At least not without a warrant."

"Which we can't get," I said.

He shook his head. "Nope."

"So now what?"

"Well," Catherine said slyly, "I might be able to get in."

"No," John and I said in concert.

"We'll figure out what happened. We don't need you putting yourself into potential danger or messing up what could turn out to be a solid relationship again," I told her.

"But..."

"No," John said again. "Let us work it out. Okay?"

She sighed. "Okay. But I hate feeling useless."

"You're never useless," I said. "We love having you here. You bring a lot to our lives every day."

"Really?" she asked, reaching for her pearls and flushing delicately. "I always feel like such a burden..."

"You are anything but," John said firmly, and I nodded, agreeing.

"You're family. And we love you."

"That's wonderful," she said, beaming. Then her face got serious. "But could you please find out whether or not he's a murderer before I try to patch things up?"

"Always a good idea," Charlene said, raising one of the

mugs and then draining what was left of it. I recalled now that I hadn't seen our Irish coffee mugs in the kitchen when we came back.

It looked like they'd found a home.

～

We tucked Charlene, who was at least three sheets to the wind, in in the cranberry room and gave Catherine the room next door—she was uncomfortable staying in the carriage house still—before checking on Gwen and Adam and heading up to our own bedroom.

"What a day," John groaned as he sank down on the bed. The cats were still with Gwen, so we had it to ourselves tonight.

"No kidding," I said, sinking down beside him and lying down, looking up at the ceiling. "I'm glad Lorraine found that envelope, but I wish the police had done a better job," I said. "How are we going to let them know it's there?"

"I figured I'd call tomorrow and ask if I can take another look."

"Do you think maybe there's some other stuff stashed there that they missed?"

"It's possible," he said. "With any luck, we'll find out."

"I'm deeply curious about Brandon, I have to admit," I said. "If it weren't for the search of the ocean floor, I'd think he was the murderer."

"The note to Steve mentioned an 'opportunity,'" John said. "Could the 'opportunity' be some kind of dirt on Brandon Marks?"

"Could be," I said. "Maybe he was offering up something about Brandon to get out of being blackmailed himself?"

"Or at least lured him there on the pretense. I hate to think about it, though; I've known Tom for years."

"Tom had a lot to lose," I said. "His family, his livelihood..."

"His freedom," John said.

"If Lorraine did the finances, there was no way he'd be able to pay a blackmailer without her knowing about it," I pointed out.

"Which is a motive for murder, for sure."

"Plus there was that new column with 'T' on it," I said.

"I thought you said it had been erased," John said.

"That's right." I sighed. "None of this makes sense, does it?"

"It doesn't," he agreed.

"We're missing something."

"Other than what Murray's hiding?" he asked.

"I think so," I said. I turned to John. "I keep thinking about Mandy. From what you know of Brandon, do you think it's possible he could have killed her?"

"Like I said, I hardly knew him. And either he doesn't recognize me or is pretending not to."

"Why come back to the island under a false name?" I asked.

"I don't know," he said. "Again, none of this makes sense."

"No," I said. "No, it doesn't."

"Maybe a good night's sleep will help jog something loose," he said.

I had my doubts, but I was tired enough not to argue. Besides, there was nothing else we could do tonight.

"I think that sounds like a great idea," I said.

"And Catherine's doctor friend is going to check out Gwen tomorrow?"

"That's the plan," I said. "And with any luck, we'll find out what happened to Tania."

"The longer she's gone, the less likely it is we'll find her," John said after a long moment.

"I know," I said. "But I'm still hoping."

16

Rain was lashing the window when the alarm went off the next morning. It had been a fitful night; I'd dreamed of money falling from the sky, and Tania trying to call but never getting through, and again, a young girl's hair waving in the dark water like seaweed, the ends caught up in a golden anchor.

I threw on a pair of jeans and a wool sweater and padded downstairs, trying not to wake anyone as I started my morning chores.

Soon, the smell of brewing coffee filled the kitchen, and I was assembling the ingredients for a breakfast casserole (gluten-free, since it used hash browns instead of bread, but not dairy-free). As I chopped onion and browned sausage in a pan, the wind whipped the trees outside, making the brilliant red leaves spiral to the ground. Fall color was gorgeous, but ephemeral; that's part of what made it such a special time of year, I reflected.

As I beat the eggs for the casserole and greased the pan, I thought through the mystery of what had happened to Mandy—and to Steve. There were obviously a ton of connections just under the surface, but I couldn't see them. Why had Brandon/Brendan chosen to come back to the island?

And had he lured Steve to his death?

I was browning sausage in a pan on the kitchen stove, filling the whole room with a lovely scent, when I heard water running upstairs. A moment later, Adam came down, wearing the same jeans and flannel he'd had on yesterday. "Can we open the windows? The smell of sausage is bothering Gwen."

"Oh, of course... sorry about that!" I said, glad I had put on a wool sweater as I opened one of the kitchen windows, letting in a gust of wet air. I put a towel down in front of the window to catch the rain; it wasn't an ideal situation, but I didn't want to make Gwen more uncomfortable. "How is she?"

"Bad again," he said, looking out the window. "I hope Catherine's friend is able to make it to the island. It's rough out there; I don't want Gwen to have to make the crossing." As he spoke, a gust of wind blew a spatter of rain into the inn. As I looked out at the water, I could see he was right; it was frosted with whitecaps. It would be a turbulent crossing—not ideal for someone with nausea.

"Did you sleep all right?" I asked.

"I did; thanks for the cot," he said. "I just wish we could get her back on track again."

"We'll get her squared away," I said, putting a note of cheery confidence into my voice. I needed to call Bridget and update her; Gwen's mom was worried. I decided to wait until we had some news to share before worrying her unnecessarily. As the sausages cooked, I grabbed a bag of frozen hash browns from the freezer and heated up more oil in a cast-iron pan. When it was hot, I put in the hash browns; soon, the smell of caramelizing potatoes joined the aroma of sausage in the kitchen. I sent a concerned look toward the stairs; I wished there was some way to keep Gwen from having to smell breakfast cooking.

"At least it isn't bacon," Adam remarked.

I laughed. "True. Want some coffee?"

"I'm going to go back up to check on her, but I'd love some."

"Help yourself," I said, nodding toward the pot.

As he poured himself a mug of coffee and looked out at the water, he asked, "Any ideas on who it was I overheard the other day? Other than Murray?"

"Our multimillionaire guest spent some time at Harvard. Maybe when he comes down for breakfast you can eavesdrop a bit?"

"If we're still here," he said. "I don't like leaving my traps so long... but I don't want to leave Gwen."

"I can take care of her today," I offered. I still hadn't asked her about the possibility of pregnancy; maybe I'd have a chance today? "I'll be around."

"It feels wrong to leave her," he said.

"We'll take care of her," I reassured him.

"I appreciate that, but I'm still going to stay," he said.

We spent a companionable ten minutes in silence as I finished making the casserole. The wind kept whipping rain into the room, and I was tempted to put a jacket on over my sweater, but keeping the windows open it was a small price to pay to keep Gwen from feeling too sick.

I had just slid the casserole into the oven when Catherine appeared, dressed in yoga pants and a long-sleeved top. "Why are the windows open?"

"Keeping the smell of sausage from making Gwen sick."

"Got it," she said, heading to the coffee pot and pouring herself a cup.

"Did you sleep okay?" I asked.

"I did," she said. "Thanks so much for letting me stay in the inn; it may be a while before I'm comfortable sleeping in the carriage house again."

"Of course," I said. "You're always welcome. Going for a jog this morning?" I asked.

"I haven't decided yet; it's a bit damp," she said, glancing out the open window at the stormy day. "How's Gwen?" she asked Adam as she stirred stevia into her coffee.

"Still not doing too hot," he said. "Do you know what time your doctor friend will be here?"

"She's planning on coming over on the noon mail boat unless I tell her differently," she said.

"Oh, that's awesome," Adam beamed, looking relieved

"I hope your friend will stay for lunch," I said.

"I hope so, too," Catherine said, sitting down at the end of the table. "I'll text her and invite her."

"I'm going to let Gwen know when she's coming," Adam said. As he disappeared up the stairs, I turned to Catherine, who was cradling her mug in both hands. "Did you get a chance to talk with Murray?"

"I called him," she said. "I'm going over there at ten; we're going to hash it out." She took a sip of coffee. "I'm nervous, but I don't know why."

"You know you're fine without him if it doesn't work out," I said. "And closure is good."

"Am I fine without him?" she asked, looking very young, suddenly, as she glanced across the kitchen at me. "I don't know. I liked having someone."

"I misspoke," I said, walking over to the table and sitting down next to her. "You're not alone. You have John, and

Gwen, and me, and everyone else on the island. If Murray is the one you want to make a life with, then great; make it work with him. If he's not, then I know you'll find someone marvelous... if you choose to."

"I hope you're right," she said.

"I know I'm right," I reassured her.

"But what if I'm wrong?" she asked. "What if Murray had something to do with what happened to that man I found beside the carriage house?"

"Is that what's bothering you?" I asked.

"I just..." She put her coffee mug down and started turning it slowly. "My intuition tells me there was something going on there. I never understood why Murray kept Steve on, and why he treated him like he did... like someone to be kept happy, somehow, not just an employee."

"What do you mean?"

"He was always asking him if he needed a drink, or a break to go to lunch... if Steve called in sick, Murray said it was no big deal."

"And that was different from how he treated other people?"

"Oh, yeah. He's such a stickler with everyone else who works for him, even if it's just a contract job. I figured they used to be friends, way back when, but when I asked him about it, he changed the subject. I never thought much about it until Steve turned up dead."

"You think Murray might have killed him?"

"I think there was something going on there. I intend to ask him today."

I didn't know what to say to that. What if Murray was a murderer? Wouldn't Catherine be putting herself in harm's way, potentially, by asking? I wasn't comfortable sending her there on her own to ask such a dangerous questions. But I couldn't exactly offer to go with her, either, under the circumstances.

"Will you come with me?" she asked. "And just stay in the van?"

"Of course," I said, relieved at this option.

"I'll take my phone with me. If it goes badly, I'll text you."

"Should we ask John to come?" I asked.

She hesitated. "No," she said. "I think I'm more comfortable with you there."

"If you're sure..."

"I'm sure," she said. "Please come."

"Happy to," I told her. "Now. How do you feel about cutting up some fruit for a fruit salad?"

"I can't very well mess that up, can I?" she asked.

I laughed. "You don't mess much up, Catherine. Melon's on the counter and there are berries in the fridge; while you do that, I'm going to whip up a batch of maple walnut coffee cake, since we ate the fudge cake yesterday." I'd come up with a recipe idea recently, and wanted to give it a try.

"Sounds good," she said as I gathered the ingredients.

It didn't take long to assemble the cake, which featured a yummy, maple-infused walnut streusel both in the middle of the cake, which was flavored with both vanilla and maple extract, and sprinkled on the top. The streusel was a mix of brown sugar and nuts, boosted with a bit of cinnamon. I popped it in next to the breakfast casserole; soon, the smell of maple joined the smell of sausage.

Poor Gwen.

As I mixed sugar and maple syrup together to make the icing, Charlene called.

"What's up?" I asked.

"Tania texted me," she said.

"Oh, thank heavens," I said, putting down the wooden spoon. "She's okay, then."

"She seems to be," Charlene said, "but I'm still worried."

"What did she say?"

"Don't worry about me, I'm fine. Can't wait to share my surprise with you.'"

"Surprise?"

"I know. Did she elope? Is she... pregnant?"

I didn't know what to say to that.

Charlene continued. "I just don't want her to throw her future away. She's so young, and has her whole future ahead of her. I've been trying to get her to go back to school and get an education, and a career... I got her to take a few correspondence classes, but she hasn't been too jazzed about them. If she went ahead and got married to some guy I've never met...."

"If her boyfriend's married, she can't elope," I pointed out.

"Unless he's a bigamist. What if he's a bigamist?"

"Let's not jump to conclusions. Have you texted her back?"

"No. What do I say?"

"Tell her you've talked to the police about filing a missing persons report," I said, "and that you want to know where she is and that she's okay. You're worried about her."

"Okay," she said. "Typing that in..." I waited as she typed. "It says it's been delivered," she said.

"Great. Now we just wait for a response."

"She'd better respond," she said.

"Call me when you hear, okay? I'll make sure my ringer's on."

"You'll tell John?"

"I will," I promised. "Let me know the moment you hear."

"I will," she promised, and hung up.

∼

Brandon Marks—or Brendan Marksburg—came down before his entourage that morning, much to my surprise. It was ten minutes before breakfast was scheduled to start, and I was putting out the coffee mugs. I'd already set out the coconut oil and stevia, along with a carafe of fresh coffee.

"Good morning," I said. "Breakfast is in a few minutes; can I get you some coffee?"

"Yes," he said, still not looking at me.

As I poured him a mug of coffee, I said, "I didn't realize until the last few days that you used to spend summers on the island."

He looked up, startled. "How did you know that?"

"Someone thought they recognized you. They looked it up." He didn't respond. "I'm surprised you came back, actually; it seemed you didn't have a great experience here."

Still no response.

"It must have been a shock to find the body of someone you knew right next to that U-Boat," I said, watching his face. There was a flicker near his right eye, but no change of expression. "Were you and Mandy close?" I pressed.

"No," he said shortly.

"Charlene tells me you wrote poems about her," I said. I didn't generally needle guests, but I needed to know if I had a murderer in my dining room. "And that she did not respond favorably."

He looked at me directly, his face expressionless. "My adolescent life is irrelevant to our relationship as customer and innkeeper," he said in a tight voice. "I'd prefer not to have a history recitation over coffee."

"I understand that," I said. "It's just... I'm surprised you didn't recognize John or Charlene."

"I have closed that chapter of my life," he said.

"Did you know Steve back then?"

"Enough," he said, slamming the mug down in front of him. Coffee splashed all over the table, but he didn't seem to notice.

"Steve was murdered. If you know anything about who might have wanted to kill him, I'd like to know," I blurted.

He arched an eyebrow and looked at me coldly. "You're a police detective now, too. Well, Detective Barnes, I'd stick to coffee if I were you. And make it stronger next time." He looked up and away, a dismissive gesture.

I didn't know what to say to that. Did his assistants know about his history on the island? I wondered. For the first time, it occurred to me that maybe Antoine had been taken along with the intent of killing Steve Batterly. But what did that have to do with what happened to Mandy? Did Brandon/Brendan suspect Steve of killing Mandy? Was it a revenge killing?

"Breakfast will be out shortly," I said in a curt voice just as Rebecca burst into the dining room.

"Mr. Marks! You were supposed to wait for me!"

"I needed coffee," he said.

"Coffee for you, too?" I asked her politely.

"Yes, please." She must have picked up on the undercurrent between her boss and me; she gave me an uneasy look before sitting down next to him.

I poured her coffee and headed back to the kitchen.

"What's wrong?" Catherine asked me.

"I just don't like rude guests," I said.

"Brandon?" she asked.

"Yup."

"I do wonder if he had something to do with what happened to Steve," Catherine commented as she rinsed the cutting board she'd used for the fruit and stood it in the dish drainer to dry.

"I do, too," I said. "The timing is too coincidental."

"So he lured Steve to the inn. The only issue with that is... why do it at the inn? That would make him more of a suspect."

"Only if someone knew of his connection with the island. Maybe he was banking on that."

"Maybe," Catherine said. "Well, I guess we'll probably never know."

Not if I had anything to do with it, I thought as I grabbed plates from the cabinet.

If Brandon Marks/Brendan Marksburg had anything to do with what had happened to Steve Batterly I planned to find out about it.

~

Catherine was ready to go right at 9:50. She looked beautiful in a cornflower-blue blouse and jeans that hugged her trim figure. A strand of pearls completed the outfit.

"You look terrific," I told her.

"You think?" she asked, a hand darting up to adjust her hair, which she'd pulled back into a chignon. A few loose strands framed her pretty face.

"He's going to melt," I assured her. "Shall we?"

"I guess it's time to get it over with," she said, and reached for the doorknob.

Anchored Inn

It was a short ride to Murray's, and very quiet. I parked in the same spot I had last time and killed the engine.

"All you're looking for is clarity," I reminded her. "Whatever happens, you'll be fine."

"If I'm not out in 30 minutes, come find me, okay?" she said.

"Of course," I told her, and reached over to give her a little hug. "I'll be right here if you need me."

She took a deep breath. "It's time," she said, and opened the van door. I watched as she walked up the driveway and rang the bell at the massive front door. Murray opened it a few seconds later, and she disappeared into the massive house, the door shutting behind her. I was pretty sure she'd be okay, but I was still nervous for her.

As I sat alone in the van, my phone rang. It was Max.

"Sorry to bother you... John gave me your number," she said. "I think my daughter spotted Charlene's niece."

"What?" I gripped the phone. "Where?"

"At U. Maine. She was walking on the other side of the quad; she was with an older man," Max said. "My daughter couldn't be sure, but does Tania own a hot pink cardigan?"

"She does," I said. "I've seen her in it at the shop. Did she talk to her?"

"She tried, but by the time she caught up to her, she and the man were in a car and driving away."

So close...

"But she wrote down the license plate," Max said. "I know it's a long shot—it probably wasn't even Tania—but it's worth a try."

"Did you tell John?" I asked.

"I did. He called the police on the mainland; they ran the plate for him, and the car belongs to a man named Dan Farland."

"Dan. The boyfriend. Your daughter is amazing... tell her thank you so much! Have they found out anything about this Dan guy?"

"They're looking him up now," she said. "We'll keep you posted."

"Does Charlene know?"

"John's on the phone with her now," she said. "He told me to tell you he'll call you the moment they find Tania."

"Thank you," I told her. "What are the odds?"

"Luck is on our side today," she said.

As I hung up and stared at Murray's front door, I hoped she was right.

17

It was a long wait. At twenty-seven minutes, I was starting to get nervous. At twenty-nine minutes, I opened the van door, prepared to march up to the front door. I had just closed it behind me when the sound of voices came from beside the house. I looked up to see Murray and Catherine rounding the corner of his mansion, both smiling. Not for the first time, I was taken aback by the juxtaposition of ruddy, stolid Murray in his polyester pants next to the graceful, stylish form of my mother-in-law.

"What are you doing here?" Murray asked, blinking.

"I was the chauffeur," I said. As curious as I was about what had happened between the two of them, I filled Catherine in on Tania first.

"That's wonderful news!" she said.

"They haven't tracked her down just yet," I reminded her.

"No, but she didn't end up like that poor girl Mandy," she said. "I was just talking to Murray about that."

"You knew who Brandon Marks was, didn't you?" I asked him.

He nodded. "Boy was an odd duck. I didn't expect him to be quite so successful. He burned down one of my office buildings, you know."

"That's why you had the file on him," I said.

"I just didn't see how someone with such terrible social skills and such a spotty record could be so successful."

Catherine looked at him and smiled. "He told me what his connection was to Steve, too," she said.

"What was that?"

"His mother used to be a housekeeper for my family," Murray said. "She raised the boy alone. Before she died, she asked me to take care of him."

"That's kind of you," I said, but remembered how he had glanced at the painting in his living room. Did I believe him?

Catherine certainly did. "I'm sorry I underestimated you," she said.

Murray snorted and shot me a look. "I'm used to it."

"His death must have been upsetting."

"It was," he said, but he didn't look terribly torn up. "We weren't friends, really, but I did feel responsible for him. He was, well, kind of my family's responsibility for a long time."

"He did other work too, though. For other families. I understand he lost a job recently."

"The Jamesons. I don't know why; their company seems to be going gangbusters. Maybe he stepped on some toes. You can ask Ed Jameson yourself; he'll be here in about ten minutes," he said. "He's coming over to do some putting with me, on the green in the back."

Of course he was. "What company?" I asked.

"They own a frozen foods company. I've been watching in the news; they recently took over a competitor, and sales seem to be skyrocketing."

"I know this seems direct," I said, "but did Steve ever try to blackmail you?"

"What? No," he said, almost too quickly. "Like I said, we were practically family."

From what I'd seen of some families, that definitely didn't preclude blackmail.

"Do you mind if we stay to meet Mr. Jameson?"

"You'll love Ed," Catherine said, linking arms with Murray as if they hadn't been separated for months. "He's such a gentleman. And he's been on the island for forever."

"Did he know about Brandon's secret identity?"

"I told him," Murray said bluntly. "Not that he cares. He never mixed with the Batterlys when he was on the island. Class differences, you know."

As he spoke, a blue Mercedes pulled up, and a younger man got out. He was handsome, with blue eyes that matched his car—and his polo shirt. He wore tan khakis and docksiders. I'd seen him a few times on the island over the years, but never spoken to him.

"Hi, Murray!" he said. "I brought a bottle we picked up in Edinburgh," he said, proffering a box of scotch, the name of which had too many consonants to pronounce.

"Thanks for coming over. I know you've met Catherine," he said, putting a hand on her elbow. "This is her daughter-in-law, Natalie. She owns the inn on the island."

"Oh, yes," he said. "The old Selfridge place. Good to see you," he said, then turned back to Murray. "Ready to hit the green?"

"I understand Steve Batterly worked for you," I said. "I'm sorry for your loss."

Ed blinked, taken aback. "What? Oh, Steve? He hasn't been with us for six months or so," he said.

"Why?" I asked.

"I don't usually discuss my household staff," he said, "and I don't like to speak ill of the dead, but his work had dropped off, and we decided he wasn't worth what we were paying."

"What kind of work did he do for you?" I asked.

"Oh, this and that," he said, but didn't meet my eyes. "He tried to get his job back... just last week, in fact. But I told him it wasn't going to work out."

I nodded. "When was that?"

"I don't recall. I lose track of time now that I'm retired." He seemed uncomfortable with the question, and was about to say something to Murray, but I didn't let him.

"I understand you knew Mandy Hoyle, too," I said.

He swallowed hard. "Everyone on the island did. She was," he chuckled, "let's just say, generous with her favors."

"Did she ever grace you with any of her favors?" I asked. "She was enamored of you, from what I understand." I wasn't sure he was the one Mandy liked, but I was fishing. And maybe I was being direct, but his comment about Mandy being "generous with her favors" rankled me.

"What?" He blushed. "I don't know what you're talking about. We barely interacted. Like I said, we ran in different circles. Are you suggesting I had something to do with that young woman's death?" he said. "I'm not the one who chained her to an anchor and pushed her overboard," he said. "Now. How about a gin and tonic, my man?" he said, clapping Murray on the back and ignoring me. "We should go out on Barb next week, by the way, now that she's out of dry dock."

"Eli get her looking good again?" Murray asked.

"Woodwork's gorgeous, just like it was when Dad had her built," Jameson said. "I was thinking of planning a picnic lunch; maybe you and Catherine can join Melissa and me sometime next week."

"I'd love that," Catherine said. "We should probably let you get to your golf."

"Dinner tomorrow night?" he asked.

"I'll be there at six," she said.

"I'll be waiting," Murray said, giving her a longing look as she walked toward the van with me in her wake.

∼

"So," I said as I backed out of the parking lot, still looking at the Mercedes. "That seemed to go well."

"Yes," she said. "I'm so glad you suggested I talk to him. It turns out it was all a big misunderstanding."

I glanced over at her; she looked happier than she had in months. "He wasn't seeing another woman?"

"Not really. He just wanted to make me jealous," she said. "He thought I'd been getting too chummy with that gentleman from Northeast Harbor... the one with the yacht. So he pretended to wine and dine this other woman."

Not exactly the foundation of a healthy relationship, if it was true, in my opinion. And if it wasn't... "How do you know he was pretending?" I asked.

"They haven't seen each other in months," she said. "He wanted to beg me to come back, but thought he'd look... I don't know. Unmanly. He says he's thought about me every day since I broke it off." She reached over and grabbed my hand. "Your advice was so good. If I hadn't talked to him... we might have gone on like that for years."

"I'm glad it's figured out," I said, "but take it easy, okay? Be careful."

She narrowed her eyes and tilted her head. "You don't believe what he told me?"

"I don't know what to believe," I said honestly. "He obviously has feelings for you. Just... I don't want you to get hurt."

"Thanks, Natalie," she said, and gave my hand another squeeze. "I think it'll be okay, but I'll be careful. I promise."

"Good. And I hope you're right," I said. As I turned onto the main road, I changed the subject. "I didn't know Murray and Ed Jameson were close."

"They've gotten together for golf talk and gin and tonics every week since Murray put in the putting green," she said. "I think they like to have someone to talk to about the financial markets and all that stuff."

"He's much younger, isn't he?"

"He's about your age, actually," she said. "His family's been on the island for ages. His mother, Barbara Leigh, had their house designed and built, and it's been in the family ever since."

"Nouveau riche?" I asked.

She nodded. "A bit flashy, kind of like Murray. I think that must be why they get along. They can compare Rolexes." She rolled her eyes, but I could tell she wasn't really bothered too much by it. "Although I think the Jamesons have much more than Murray ever will; that's why Ed can play golf all the time. Not that I care; he's got more than enough as it is." She turned to me. "How do you know Mandy had a crush on him?"

"I've been asking around," I said. "She was looking for a wealthy Prince Charming to sweep her off her feet. Charlene told me that for a few weeks, anyway, she was hoping Ed would play the role nicely."

"I do remember her being boy-crazy," she said, and gave

me a sidelong look. "You know she and John went out briefly, right?"

"That's what everyone keeps telling me," I said. "But that was a very long time ago."

"He was upset when she just vanished. The whole island was, though, really."

Even though that was years ago and John was now my husband, I still felt a flare of jealousy. "It wasn't serious between them, was it?" John had told me it wasn't, but for some reason, I wanted to hear it from Catherine, too.

"I think he did like her at first, but he was the one who broke up with her at the end of the summer. She wanted him to write every day. She was... clingy. Needy, I guess."

"Ah," I said. "Do you know if she and Ed ever hung out?"

"Not that I know of," she said. "He and the Karstadt boy mainly kept to themselves. They ran with some of the rich kids who summered on the mainland, for the most part. Ed's dad had just bought a big sailboat and named it after his wife, Barbara Leigh, so they spent a lot of time on that."

"That's the boat Ed was talking about; he calls it Barb, right?"

"Right," she said. "You can see it moored in the harbor."

"Did either of them know Steve at all?" I asked on a hunch.

"Probably a little bit. Steve's father made his money the same way Steve did; he did handyman jobs for folks around the island, and took Steve along as his apprentice, so to speak. Steve never did finish high school; he took over for his dad and never left the island."

Something about Ed Jameson bothered me all the way home.

But it wasn't until I was back at the inn that I realized what it was.

"I've got one more errand to do," I said as I dropped Catherine off at the inn. "I just remembered; I'll be back soon."

"Want company?"

"No," I said. "I shouldn't be long."

"I'll do a last check on the rooms," she told me, then leaned over and kissed me on the cheek, which was a total surprise. "Thank you so much for encouraging me to talk to Murray. I'm so... happy," she beamed. She got out of the van and practically danced up to the kitchen door.

As I headed back up the driveway a minute later, I found myself hoping I'd done the right thing... and not just made things worse.

18

It was only a few minutes before I pulled up outside of Steve Batterly's cottage. It looked to be a two-or-three bedroom place, with a freshly paved driveway. Although the grass was slightly overgrown, the siding had recently been painted, and a few fresh planks on the front porch indicated recent repairs. I parked in one of the two spaces at the top of the driveway and got out, eyeing the place.

I walked around to the back of the house, hoping to find a door. Fortunately, I was in luck. Up a few wooden steps was a door with a half-window. I climbed the steps and tried the knob. The door was locked, but when I lifted the doormat, I found a key, and a moment later I was standing inside Steve's spartan kitchen.

The cabinets were oak, and the floor linoleum—clean, but dated. I tried to recall everything I'd seen on crime shows with John, and began in the freezer; I didn't know what I was looking for, but I had a feeling there was something here that would tell me what had happened to the former handyman.

There was no exciting container hidden in the back of the freezer. All I found was a bottle of Stoli and a stack of TV dinners. The fridge was much the same way: empty save for two wrinkled apples and a six-pack of Bud Lite.

I found nothing in the kitchen, so moved on to the living room, which was outfitted with an enormous projector TV and what looked like surround-sound speakers, along with a huge leather sectional. None of which was cheap; Steve must have been doing pretty well for himself. I wondered how much of this had been funded by the numbers Lorraine had found on the note under the floor.

Speaking of the floor, I found myself paying close attention to the hardwood planks underfoot. I spent a good twenty minutes testing all of them and then looking behind the vintage pin-up girl poster on the wall above the couch, but found no sign of anything unusual.

I moved down the hall to the two bedrooms and the bathroom. In the guest bedroom, a board squeaked as I walked around the bed. I knelt down and felt for a wobble; sure enough, there was a mark at the end of the board where it looked like something had scraped the wood repeatedly. I pulled a pocket knife from my back pocket and pried it up.

Although John had called the mainland to tell them about the loose floorboard, the detectives evidently hadn't gotten around to following up on what Lorraine had told us; sure enough, the board hid a secret compartment of sorts. Lorraine had evidently returned what she found; in a gap beneath the board was the list she'd shown me the other day, along with the neat stack of bills. I felt around to see if she'd missed anything before replacing the board. I walked around the rest of the room, looking for another board with signs of having been pried up before. Nothing in this room, but when I went into the master bedroom, I noticed another strangely scuffed board under the night stand next to the neatly made queen-sized bed.

I pushed the night stand aside and retrieved my knife, slipping it under the end of the board.

Sure enough, there was a stack of envelopes.

I pulled it out, curious to see what Steve had collected. The first envelope was labeled T. I opened it to find pictures of Tom Lockhart with a young woman, holding hands and exchanging a kiss on a city street that looked like it might be Portland, based on the red brick.

So blackmail it was.

I was about to open the second envelope when a door creaked down the hall. I shoved the envelopes back into the hole and hurriedly slid the board back into place. I couldn't get it level; part of it still stuck up, but footsteps were already in the kitchen, so I abandoned it. I picked up the nightstand and set it down close to where it had been, then dropped to the floor and slid myself under the bed, hoping whoever it was wouldn't see me.

As I peered out from under the low-slung bed, a pair of docksiders approached down the hallway.

I recognized them from earlier.

It was Ed Jameson.

He stopped at the bedroom door, surveying the out-of-place night stand, no doubt. "I know you're in here," he said in a calm, sing-song voice that made my stomach turn over. "You can't hide from me." As I watched, the docksiders padded to the closet. He opened the door and peered inside, then stepped back out. I held my breath, praying he wouldn't bend down and look under the bed. He didn't. Instead, he left the bedroom and walked down the hall.

I took the opportunity to slide out from under the bed as

quietly as I could. I was about to sprint down the hall when his footsteps came closer. I ran into the closet, trying to hide behind a row of hanging shirts, but the floor creaked as I moved.

Jameson was back in the bedroom in an instant, and it didn't take long for him to get to the closet.

"I knew you were in here," he said as he flipped the light back on. "Come out so I can see you."

I slid the knife out from my back pocket and opened it, holding it behind my back, then stepped out from behind the shirts.

"What are you doing here, Natalie Barnes?" he asked. The way he said "Barnes" was pure Boston. The hair on the back of my neck stood straight up.

"Just looking around," I said.

"Looking for what?"

"My friend's niece is missing," I said, because it was the first thing that popped into my head. "I was wondering if it had anything to do with what happened to Steve, because of the timing," I babbled. "I guess I was looking for a lead."

He cocked an eyebrow at me. "Find anything?"

"No, unfortunately," I said. "What are you doing here?"

"I had a feeling about you," he said. He was a big man, I noticed; I could try to slip out, but if he caught me, I could tell it wouldn't go well. "You seemed very curious about what happened to Mandy."

"I am," I said, glancing at the doorway and wondering if I could make a break for it. "My husband used to date her."

"She dated everyone on the island, believe me. Why don't you step out of the closet?" he asked, his eyes scanning everything.

"Sure," I said, and almost brushed against him as I stepped out into the bedroom.. His eyes noted the night table, which was askew. "What's this?" he asked. He opened the drawer and rifled through it, then shut it. I was almost sure I was out of the woods when he noticed the board. As I watched, he dropped to a squat and pulled it up, revealing the envelopes hidden inside. I started sidling toward the door.

"I wouldn't do that if I were you," he said, glancing at me sidelong. I froze. "I was a track star. I'd catch you before you got to the front door."

I stopped moving, but started thinking. Was there something I could bean him with? I was too far from the lamp to grab it and hit him with it. I scanned the room for alternative weapons, but came up empty. I had the knife, but could I stick it in someone's back? I wasn't sure I was up to it.

"Interesting," he said, removing the stack and standing up. "You found these, didn't you?"

"No," I lied.

"Right." I could tell he didn't believe me. "Let's see what's in these."

He flipped through the envelopes until he found the one marked "EJ." Inside was a paper-clipped stack of news clippings and a photograph. I couldn't see what it was, but his eyes narrowed as he saw it, and he looked at me in a new, speculative way.

"What are the clippings?" I asked.

"You already know," he said. "You knew the moment I slipped up earlier and mentioned the chain."

I swallowed. He was right; nobody knew that Mandy had been chained to the killick.. It wasn't visible on the footage, and only the investigators and John knew that that's how she had been fastened to it.

Ed had killed Mandy all those years ago, either accidentally or on purpose, and I was guessing Steve witnessed it and/or helped him get rid of the body. "You can't sail the Barbara Leigh with just one person, can you?" I asked.

"You can't," he agreed. "And we couldn't use the skiff. Too dangerous if we got stopped."

"What happened, anyway?"

"She came over to the house, dressed all sexy. We had a few drinks, and she got friendly."

"Friendly," I said.

"You know what I mean. I assumed she wanted to get busy—she was all over me—but she changed her mind halfway through. We were kind of wrestling, and she accidentally hit her head on the corner of the night stand. I tried to wake her up, but she was gone."

Accidentally. For some reason, I found that hard to believe. "And you got Steve to help you?"

"You pegged it," he said. "We came to terms. We used bolt cutters to get the killick—it was the only thing we could think of we could attach to her to to get her to sink. He helped me get her out to the boat; we put her in a storage compartment with the killick; and Steve brought some chain from his father's workshop. It was done in an hour, and he never said a word about it to anyone."

"And you made payments all these years. Until recently."

"It seemed pointless after a certain amount of time, and he was just asking too much. There was no body, and who was going to believe him, after all these years?"

"Until Brandon found Mandy's body."

"Crazy, right? I mean, what are the odds? Unless he was looking for her all those years; he carried a torch for her, that's for sure."

"So Steve came to you for more money."

"Of course. Steve was ready to cash in. Wanted five thousand a month for life to keep his mouth shut." He snorted. "Ridiculous."

"So you lured him to the inn and killed him with Tom's kitchen knife," I said. I'd already guessed that Jameson was responsible for Mandy's death, or at least mixed up in it, but I was still not sure about Steve... so I was fishing.

"Nobody locks doors on this island. It was easy."

"Why at the inn?" I asked.

"It was about as far away from me as you could get," he answered, confirming my suspicions. "Plus, with good old Brendan on the island, it was a good way to deflect suspicion."

"Which is why you signed the letter T.L."

"I heard about their little dust-up." He glanced down at the envelopes. "Apparently our selectman was getting a little busy off the clock. I imagine Steve offered to keep quiet about it, in exchange for a little extra green."

"Was he blackmailing anyone else?" I asked.

"The Karstadts," he said. "He found out Mrs. Karstadt had a nice bit on the side, apparently. He agreed to keep quiet if she kept him busy... with jobs around the house and a little extra on the side. Your mother-in-law's boyfriend also had him on the payroll."

"Murray? Why?" I asked.

"Didn't get to that envelope yet?" he asked. "Oh, my good buddy had a bit of a cocaine habit a while back. Steve found out about it and took a few pics of him doing lines on the kitchen counter. Murray didn't want word getting out, so he gave Steve a regular job and some extra money under the table."

"Does he still use it?"

"The extra money?"

"The cocaine," I said.

"I think he picked it up again not long ago," he said. "He was off it for a while when he was seeing your hubby's mom, but since they broke off..."

"Wonderful," I groaned.

"I can see that would be upsetting. But you've got bigger issues than that right now."

I did. But Ed Jameson was unarmed. And I wasn't. I reached behind me and pulled my phone from one pocket. Before Ed could say anything, I unlocked the phone with my finger and said, "Call John."

"What?" Ed asked.

Not long after he spoke, the phone said, "Calling John." Then there was silence.

"Give me your phone," Ed demanded.

I brandished the knife and pressed the phone to my ear. It was still ringing.

As I held my breath, it went to voicemail. Crap.

"You don't want to do that," Ed said, advancing on me.

"...Please leave a message and I'll get back to you..." the phone was saying. Finally, it beeped.

"John, I'm at Steve's place, and Ed Jameson..." Ed lurched toward me, knocking the phone away and sending it skittering under the bed.

I jabbed with the knife and he backed up a few steps. "Ed Jameson killed Mandy and Steve and he's attacking me!" I yelled, hoping the phone was still picking up the message.

"Shut up!" Ed snarled, lunging again. I spun to the right and jabbed; I caught his forearm, and a line of red appeared. He jerked back and swore.

"Please come help me!" I yelled. "I'm at Steve's and Ed is going to kill me! He knew Mandy was chained to the killick... Steve helped him get rid of her body... please come help!"

Ed hurled himself at me, grabbing the hand with the knife and wrenching it until the knife rattled on the floor.

"Now I'm going to have to kill your husband, too," he said. "Or at least go get his phone. Damn it, woman. Why didn't you just leave well enough alone?"

He reached for the lamp on the night stand and raised it above his head. As he did, I kneed him in the crotch and stamped on his foot.

Ed gasped and let go of my hand. I pushed past him and ran down the hall to the front door, fumbling in my pocket for the van keys; I could already hear Ed pounding down the hall behind me. I pushed through the back door and ran around the house; I didn't know if the front door was unlocked, and didn't want to take the time to test it.

As I rounded the front corner of the house, Ed burst through the front door. I raced to the van, opening the door and slamming it shut. Before I could lock it, though, he grabbed the handle and wrenched the door open.

"No!" I yelled, jamming the key into the ignition and turning it. I threw the van into reverse and hit the gas as Ed reached in. The door hit him in the shoulder, but he didn't give up. As he reached for me, I wrenched the steering wheel to the right. He stumbled and fell away as the van's back bumper cracked into a tree, jerking the van to a stop. Before he had a chance to regroup, I pulled the door shut and threw the van into drive, veering around him as I pulled away from the house. The side view mirror clipped him in the chest as I tore out of the driveway and headed for the inn, my heart pounding in my chest.

19

John was already sprinting up the driveway, phone to his ear, when I crested the hill above the inn.

When he saw me, relief washed across his face, but he didn't stop running until he got to the van.

"I just got your message... are you okay?"

"I'm okay," I said, "but he wants to kill both of us. Did you call the mainland police?"

"I did," he said. "They're on their way in a launch."

"Not the helicopter?"

"Budget cuts," he said.

"We have to get into the inn," I said. "He's coming."

Sure enough, behind me, I could hear the roar of the Mercedes' engine.

John sprinted around the side of the van and vaulted into the passenger seat. "Drive," he said as I hit the gas, racing down to the inn.

I pulled up to a stop about ten feet from the inn with Ed's Mercedes practically on the van's back bumper; we didn't have the horsepower to match him.

"What now?" I asked John.

"Just stay put," he said as Ed threw open the door of the Mercedes and strode up to the van. Only now, he had a gun in his hand.

"He's armed," I said in a hoarse whisper. "What do we do?"

"We'll stay calm and try to talk reason," John said. A moment later, a bullet ricocheted off the side mirror, shattering it.

"Reason?" I asked.

I hadn't turned the van off. I glanced out at Ed, who was about to reach the driver's side door, then threw the van in reverse and gunned it.

The back bumper smacked into the Mercedes. Ed, who was now in front of the van, stared at me, his mouth an "O" of surprise, then raised the gun. Before he had a chance to shoot, I wrenched the steering wheel to the left, hit the gas again, and ran over him.

∼

"OH MY GOD," I breathed when the van rolled to a stop. The thump of his body hitting the van seemed to echo in my head. "I just ran someone over."

"That was quick thinking," John said.

"Is he okay?" I asked, shuddering at the thought of what I'd done. I hadn't felt the tires go over him, but I knew he'd gone down when the front grille hit him.

"I highly doubt it," John remarked, "but I'll check. Stay here."

"Right," I croaked as John opened the passenger door slowly, crouching down as he stepped out of the car. I watched with my heart in my throat as he disappeared around the front of the van.

"He's still alive," John called. "But he's unconscious; it looks like he hit his head on the pavement when he went down. Call the EMTs; they're going to want to take him in."

"Thank God," I breathed, saying a small prayer of thanks that I hadn't killed the man. He might be a murderer, but I didn't want his—or anyone else's—blood on my hands.

Besides, there'd been enough death on the island to last a lifetime already.

20

"So after all this time, it was someone local," Charlene said as we sat in my kitchen later that day. She'd closed the store to come and be with me; John was still talking with the police, and I was shaken. Ed Jameson had gone to the hospital on the mainland with some broken ribs, a broken leg, and a concussion. The wheels had missed him, thankfully, so I didn't have to spend the rest of my life knowing I'd killed someone.

"Weird to think about, isn't it? I still feel bad about running him over."

"He was going to shoot you and John," she said, pushing back a stray lock of hair. Although she was beautiful no matter what, she hadn't put on make-up since Tania disappeared, and there were still circles around her eyes. "What else were you going to do?"

"I guess you're right," I said. As I took another sip of my coffee, I heard voices upstairs. "I wonder how it's going up there?"

"We'll find out soon, I'm guessing," Charlene said as footsteps sounded from the top of the stairs.

I looked up to see Catherine's friend, Doctor Castello, followed by a stunned-looking Adam.

"Uh oh," I said, feeling my heart clutch. "What's wrong?"

"I'll let Adam tell you that," Doctor Castello said, turning to my young nephew-in-law.

"Gwen's... well... we're pregnant," he said, still looking like he didn't quite believe it himself.

"Pregnant?" I said, standing up as a thrill of excitement passed through me. "That's wonderful! Is she going to be okay?"

"She needs to drink more," the physician said. "I gave her some anti-nausea meds. If they don't work, we'll have to check her in and give her an IV. I'll come by tomorrow and see how it's working; if she's not better, I'm going to recommend she go to the hospital."

"When is she due?" Charlene asked.

"I'm estimating mid-April," the doctor said. "We'll know more when she has a sonogram."

"A spring baby," Charlene said. "I can't believe it. Natalie, you're going to be an aunt again!"

"And you're going to be a father," I said to Adam, who was still looking stunned, but with an enormous smile on his face. "This calls for celebration," I announced, and then saw Charlene's face. She was still missing Tania.

"She's in contact with us; we'll find her," I encouraged her in a low voice. "Are you up for a bit of bubbly?"

"I'm always up for bubbly," Charlene said, but her eyes were haunted.

I retrieved the bottle of Prosecco I kept in the back of the fridge for celebratory emergencies and distributed glasses. "Wait... I need to get John!" I realized. "Hold that thought." I hurried to the parlor to retrieve John, who was wrapping things up with the detectives. "We've got news," I told him.

He stood up, a furrow between his brows. "Is it Gwen? Is she okay?"

"I'll let Adam tell you," I said, grabbing his hand. "I'll bring him back in a few," I told the detectives. "Promise."

"What's going on?" he asked as I led him into the kitchen. "Is it serious?" It took him a moment to register the Prosecco and the glasses. "Wait... what is this about?"

"Adam?" I said.

"We're pregnant," he announced, his face splitting into a smile.

"You're... Gwen's... oh! That's wonderful!!!" John said, walking over and pulling Adam into a big hug. "You'll be terrific parents. Is she okay?" he asked as he released the young lobsterman.

"The good doctor here gave her some anti nausea meds. We're going to try to get her hydrated... if not, we'll take her in and get an IV into her, but apparently she should be okay."

"The baby's due in April," I said as I popped the Prosecco bottle.

"A spring surprise," John beamed. "I can't wait to meet her... or him!"

As he spoke, I glanced at Charlene. She had a smile on, but I could tell she was upset.

"She'll be back," I said.

"I hope you're right," she said, taking a small sip of Prosecco and trying to look cheerful.

21

We weren't the only ones celebrating with bubbly that day, as it turned out. Although Brandon Marks went for Dom Perignon instead of ten-dollar Prosecco.

"Do you have any snacks we can have?" Rebecca asked as I gathered glasses for the celebration. The U-Boat had been positively identified. Evidently it had been sunk by what appeared to have been a destroyer. Several major newspapers were sending up reporters to cover the story—the submersible was going to do more exploratory work—and the German government had been notified of the find.

"I've got some Marcona almonds, some gluten-free crackers and some Gouda. Will that work?"

"Sounds perfect," she said. "And bring a glass for yourself Mr. Quinton," she told John.

I assembled a quick snack board and brought both John and an extra glass into the dining room, joining Brandon, Rebecca, and Antoine, along with much of the crew of the research vessel.

"First," Brandon said, "to the success of the expedition.

We found a vessel that had been lost for more than 70 years, uncovering a piece of history. Congratulations to Maureen and the team." Maureen smiled proudly as we all raised our glasses.

"And to you, Mr. Marks, for funding the research!" she replied before we drank. We all took a sip—the champagne was dry and tangy and zingy all at once—before Brandon spoke again, this time with a more serious tone. "Perhaps more importantly, to the lost men of U-Boat 809, and to the scores of lost lives they caused," Brandon said solemnly, lifting his glass. "And, more personally... to Mandy Hoyle," he added, his voice cracking slightly as he pronounced her name. For the first time, I saw pain in his eyes. "My first love," he said hoarsely. "I'm sorry it ended so tragically."

We all raised our glasses again, the smiles faded, and toasted to the lives of those lost. Then, after a solemn moment of silence, the conversation began.

"How did you identify the wreck, anyway?" John asked the scientist.

"We did a radar scan of the sea floor," she informed him. "The U-Boat was in a bit of a trench, so previous scans didn't catch it; I'm thrilled we were able to find it. It was almost as if it wanted to be found."

Or Mandy did, I thought, taking another sip of my champagne and glancing out toward the carriage house where Steve Batterly had met his end. He'd kept his secret for decades. What other secrets had he had? I still needed to tell Catherine about Murray's habit... and I now knew more than I wanted to about Tom Lockhart. It wasn't my place to say anything, but my heart ached for Lorraine. Who else had Steve been blackmailing? I wondered.

I wasn't sure I wanted to know.

As I pondered these somber thoughts, Charlene burst into the dining room.

"What's wrong?" I asked, praying it wasn't bad news about Tania.

"She's back!" Charlene said. "She came back on the 2:00 mail boat!"

"She's okay?"

"Fit as a fiddle, but I'm still tempted to take a piece out of that girl's hide."

"Oh, that's fabulous news," I said, feeling my whole body relax with relief. "Did she tell you what happened?"

"She spent the last few days in Orono, just like the Instagram photos said. Turns out she's going to the University of Maine on a full scholarship in the spring," Charlene said, a proud smile on her face.

"What? That's wonderful!" I said, sweeping my friend into a hug. "Is that what she was doing?"

"She was," Charlene said. "Turns out Dan was one of her professors. He pulled some strings at U. Maine to get her extra funding; she was there this weekend staying in one of the dorms and interviewing for scholarship opportunities."

"So she didn't elope with a married man after all," I said. "Thank goodness! But next time, a little more communication wouldn't go amiss!"

"No kidding," Charlene said. "I'm still furious with her, though. I know she was trying to surprise me, but just vanishing like that... I told her she can never, ever do that again. What was she thinking?"

"She wasn't," I said. "We didn't either, at that age."

"I know." Charlene sighed. "I keep thinking of poor Mandy... I know they arrested Ed Jameson, but what happened?"

I filled her in on everything that had happened that day so far.

"So you ran him over?"

"I did," I said.

"He deserved it," she said. "Who does something like that? Poor Mandy... she had such high hopes, and it all came to that. And Steve knew all along... how do you keep something like that quiet?"

"I think the money helped," I commented.

"I guess... what a rotten way to make a living. I think I've lost five pounds in the last week, though, so it's not all bad. Although I'm going to need to find some extra help at the store..."

"There's maple cake in the kitchen if you want to balance out your calorie deficit," I said, wishing I could get Gwen to eat a slice. "I still can't believe I'm going to be a great-aunt."

"It's going to be amazing! They'll be such good parents... and you'll have a new niece to read stories to, and bake with..."

"Or nephew," John pointed out.

"Whichever," Charlene said. "We still need to celebrate. Is there any of that champagne left?"

"You are feeling better, aren't you?" I said, laughing.

"Much better," she said. "And I'll take you up on that cake!" she added with a grin.

~

ALL IN ALL, it was a good day. I was wrapping up a few business details at the front desk when Max and Ellie came in the front door. Max's eyes were shining, and her cheeks were pink. "I heard you had an exciting day!"

"What do you mean?"

"I just ran into your friend Eleazer... he told me you caught the killer!"

"If by 'caught' you mean 'ran over,' then I guess that's true," I said. "I'm glad to get it all wrapped up. I'm sad about Mandy, but at least her family has closure."

"And it sounds like the man who died wasn't exactly a prize package either," Ellie commented. "Still... it's sad."

"It is," I agreed, feeling a twinge again for poor Mandy. "But you look happy," I said to Max. "What's up?"

"Ellie and I just had a long talk, and the two of you talked me into it," she said. "I'm going to buy a bookstore!"

"That's wonderful!" I said. "Where?"

"I don't know," she said, "but I'm going to talk to Loretta and see if she'll sell the store in Snug Harbor to me. I can't stand to think of it going downhill, and I'd love to keep it alive for future generations. I just hope I can afford it!"

"Like I said, I can help finance it if you like," Ellie offered.

Max turned to her. "Are you sure?"

"I'm sure," she said. "I think you're going to be a smashing success."

"I can't believe I'm going to do this. I'm a little scared, honestly," she admitted. "It's a big step."

"Anything worth doing is scary," I said. "Oh... and thank you so much for your help with Tania. You were right; your daughter did see her!"

Max's smile faded, and her eyes got round. "Is she okay?"

"She's fine. In fact, she'll be at the U of Maine with your daughter next semester. She spent the last few days talking with financial aid officers and looking at the dorms; she didn't tell Charlene because she wanted to surprise her. She worked so hard on her correspondence courses and did so well on her SATs that they're giving her a full ride."

"A full ride? That's wonderful!" Max said. "All kinds of good news today!"

"So all's well that ends well," Ellie said.

"For most of us, anyway," I said, thinking of Mandy. "There's some more good news, though; my niece is going to have a baby!"

"That's wonderful. Congratulations, Aunt Natalie!" Max said, grinning.

"A day of new beginnings," said Ellie. "New store, new college career, and a new baby in the family."

"Life is pretty good, isn't it?" I said.

"There are some rough patches," Max agreed, "but yes. There's plenty of good if you look for it. And always a chance for a new chapter."

As I looked at Max, her sad face now full of life and hope, I had to agree.

And I couldn't wait to see what she wrote in her own next chapter.

AND SPEAKING OF NEXT CHAPTERS... read on for the first chapter of A KILLER ENDING: A Seaside Cottage Books Mystery, the first of the new Snug Harbor Mysteries featuring Max Sayers!

SNEAK PREVIEW: A KILLER ENDING

Two years ago, if you'd told me I'd be spending my 42nd birthday driving north on I-95 with all of my worldly possessions hitched to my Honda CRV in a U-Haul trailer like some sort of oversize snail shell, I'd have told you you were crazy.

But things change.

Boy, do they change.

It wasn't the best time to head out of Boston. I hadn't gotten the last picture of my two darling girls packed up into a box and loaded into the back of the trailer until just after four o'clock on Friday afternoon. Since it was the first weekend of summer vacation in Massachusetts, I was now trapped on the highway with several thousand fellow motorists, many of them with kayaks or bicycles strapped to the backs of their SUVs. Like a lot of them, I was headed north to the Maine coast to enjoy a sunny, sparkling summer weekend. Unlike them, however, I didn't plan to come back on Sunday.

Or at all.

Just three months earlier, listening to a deep gut instinct

for the first time in almost two decades, I'd signed a stack of paperwork, plunked down my life savings, and purchased my very own bookstore, Seaside Cottage Books, in Snug Harbor, Maine. With the help of an assistant, I'd spent the last several weeks clearing out years of debris from the storage room, dusting the shelves, taking stock of the inventory, and using what little money I had left to add a carefully curated selection of new books. I'd also spent a good bit of time redecorating the place, rolling up my sleeves and repainting the walls a gorgeous blue, making new, nautical-print cushions for the window seats with my mother's old sewing machine, and scouring second-hand stores for the perfect cozy armchairs to tuck away in corners.

The grand re-opening celebration was scheduled for tomorrow night, and I was as nervous as… well, as nervous as a middle-age, recently divorced woman who's just spent everything she has on a risky venture in a small Maine town can be. I'd used my final pennies (and a small loan) to take out ads in the local paper and spread flyers all over town; I hoped my marketing efforts worked.

From his crate behind me, Winston, my faithful Bichon-mystery-mix rescue, whined. I reached back to put my fingers through the grate and pat his wooly white head; he licked my fingers. "I know, buddy. But once we get there, you'll get to go for walks on the beach and sniff all kinds of things. I promise you'll love it." He let out a whimper, but settled down.

Walks on the beach. Fresh sea air. A business that allowed me to be my own boss. A home to call my own. I repeated these sentences like a mantra, as if they could wipe the memory of the complicated and painful last year-and-a-half from my mind and my soul.

Move forward, Max. Just move forward.

I took a deep breath and let my foot off the brake unconsciously. The car rolled forward and I slammed on the brake again, just in time to avoid rear-ending the Highlander in front of me, which had four bikes strapped to the back. Two adult bikes, and two smaller, pink and blue sparkly bikes, one of which had pink ribbons trailing from the handlebar grips. Two daughters. My eye was drawn to the heads in the car; a happy family, going to Maine for the summer. A dull pain sprouted in my chest, but once again, I banished it.

Forward, Max.

~

By the time I reached the exit for Snug Harbor, the sun was low in the sky and my stomach was growling. I glanced back at Winston, who was still giving me a reproachful look from his dark brown eyes.

"We're almost there," I promised him.

I turned at the exit. Within moments, we'd left the impersonal, clogged highway behind and were heading down a winding rural route, passing handmade signs offering firewood for sale, a sea glass souvenir shop, and a log-cabin-style restaurant advertising early-bird lobster dinners and senior specials. I hooked a left at a T-intersection marked by a large planter filled with dahlias and white salvia. And then, as if I had crossed the threshold into another world, I was in Snug Harbor.

In the rearview mirror, I could see Winston perk up as I tooled down Main Street, which was already buzzing with summer visitors, and when I opened the windows and let the cool, fresh sea breeze in, he sat up and started sniffing. Quaint, homegrown shops faced the narrow, car-lined street, which was landscaped with trees and flower-filled planters. Business appeared to be booming; a line snaked out the door of Scoops Ice Cream, Judy's Fudge Emporium was hopping, and lots of relaxed-looking families strolled the streets with ice cream cones and dreamy smiles. Live guitar music drifted out of the Salty Dog Pub as we rolled by, and I caught a whiff of fried clams that made my mouth water. I'd have to splurge on dinner out soon, I told myself. I just hoped a lot of those vacationers were looking for good reads to relax with on their hotel and rental-house porches so I could support my deep-fried seafood habit.

As I crested the gentle hill, passing the town green on my left, the street in front of me seemed to fall away, leaving a perfectly framed view of Snug Harbor.

The water was a beautiful, deep blue, and beyond it nestled the pristine, tree-clad Snug Island; the tide was low, so the sandbar connecting the Snug Harbor to the small island across the water was visible. As I rolled down the street, the whale-watching boat came into view; the big white vessel was just pulling out for its sunset tour, and beyond, I could see the four masts of the Abigail Todd as it sailed out of the harbor toward the small, outlying islands.

It took my breath away, just as it had the first time I'd seen it more then thirty years ago.

I drove down to the end of main street and the pier, which was filled with a mix of working boats and pleasure boats (including a few large yachts), then turned left on Cottage Street.

I passed three dockside restaurants featuring lobster boils and fisherman's dinners, catching yet more whiffs of fried clams (this was going to be an occupational hazard), the cobalt harbor peeking out between the buildings and snow-white seagulls calling and whirling overhead in the evening light. There was a little blue-painted shop called

Ivy's Seaglass and Crafts, which I knew housed an eclectic assortment of local jewelry and artwork, and then, on its own, a little ways down the street, the walkway flanked by pink rosebushes... Seaside Cottage Books.

My new home... in fact, my new life.

I looked at the familiar Cape-style building with fresh eyes, admiring the gray-shingled sides of the little house, the white curtains in the upper windows, the pots of red geraniums looking fresh and sprightly in half-barrels on the freshly painted porch. Two rockers with handmade cushions awaited readers. Behind it, I knew, a beach-rose-lined walkway led down to a rocky beach; a beach Winston and I would be able to walk every morning, greeting the sun. And the bookstore itself—it was a dream come true for me. A place where I could connect with other people who loved books, and introduce others to literary treasures that would open up their minds and their worlds.

Pride surged in me at the sight of the book display that graced one of the sparkling front windows—a hand-selected variety of Maine-centric books and beloved reads, including several of Lea Wait's delightful Maine mysteries, two books by Sarah Orne Jewett, a whimsical book by two young women who had hiked the Appalachian Trail barefoot, and —a personal favorite for years—Bill Bryson's *A Walk in the Woods*. They were like old friends welcoming me home, even though I'd just left my home of twenty years for the last time this morning. I smiled, feeling a surge of hope for the first time that day. A sign with the words OPEN SOON was hooked on the door, and I found myself envisioning the community of readers who would gather here.

Goose bumps rose on my arms as I pulled into the gravel drive beside the small building, carefully easing in the trailer behind me so as not to knock over the mailbox. I parked next to the rear of the house, so that it would be a short trip from the trailer to the back door of the shop. And the back door of my home, which was an apartment on the second floor with a cozy bedroom, a small kitchen and living area, a view of the harbor, and even a balcony on which I planned to put a rocking chair and enjoy my morning coffee, as soon as I could afford it.

My store.

My home.

It was the first time in my whole life I'd had something that was completely and totally mine, and I told myself in that moment that I'd do anything to keep anyone else from taking it away from me.

Of course, at the time, I had no idea someone would try quite so soon.

Like tomorrow.

∽

"Hey, Max!"

As I clambered out of the Honda, a bright-faced young woman opened the back door of the shop and stepped out to meet me.

"What are you still doing here?" I asked.

"Just finishing up a few last minute things for the big opening tomorrow," she said. "My mom lent us some platters for cookies, I borrowed two coffee percolators from Sea Beans, and I've got a line on a punch bowl, too."

"You're amazing," I said, smiling. Bethany had been my right-hand woman in getting the bookstore up and running. She'd been crushed when the previous owner, Loretta Satterthwaite, became too ill to carry on with the store, and had banged on the front door two days after I bought the shop. I'd greeted her with cobwebs in my hair—I'd been dusting—and she talked me into an "internship."

"Snug Harbor needs a bookstore," she'd said. "Plus, I plan to be a writer, so I need to keep up with happenings in the industry."

"What about the library?"

"Their budget for new books is meager. I've volunteered there for years," she told me, "but Snug Harbor without a Seaside Books... it's like having a body without a heart." Since I felt much the same way—I'd spent many summer days holed up in the shop as a girl—I felt an immediate kinship. She smiled, and I noticed the freckles dotting her nose and the bright optimism in her fresh-scrubbed, young face. She reminded me of my daughters, Audrey and Caroline, and my heart melted a little bit. "I'll start as an intern; once the store opens, we'll figure something out. I live with my parents and I'm only taking classes part-time. I've got both ample time and a scholarship."

"I can't pay you much," I warned her. "I'm not opening for months and I spent almost everything on the building."

"I'm sure we'll come to a suitable arrangement," she'd announced, peering past me at a jumble of books the previous owner had left on a table. "I'll start by rescuing those poor books from their current condition," she'd informed me, and walked right into the store—and into my life.

Thank heavens for angels like Bethany.

Now, as I stood outside Seaside Cottage Books the day before the grand opening, the sight of a cheerful Bethany in jeans and a pink flannel shirt lifted my heart.

"How's it going in there?" I asked.

"Everything's ship-shape," she announced. "I've got the Maine section finished up—two local authors dropped their books by today—and I picked up more coffee and creamer, and some hot chocolate for the little ones."

"Terrific," I said, feeling better already. "Give me the receipts, and I'll reimburse you!" I opened the back door of the SUV and picked up Winston's crate, setting it on the ground. "There is one thing, though," Bethany said.

"Oh?"

"A rather insistent woman has stopped by three times today," she informed me as I liberated Winston from his crate.

"Who?" I asked as my fluffy little dog shook himself all over and trotted over to greet Bethany. He'd been my faithful companion since I'd retrieved him from the pound, covered in mange and painful-looking sores and looking a little like a scabby goat, six years ago. With lots of TLC and medication, we'd taken care of the mange and sores, along with the worms and other maladies that had kept him curled up on the couch with me the first few months. Now, he was bouncy, curious, and suffering from a bit of a Napoleon complex, particularly (alas) with dogs that were more than ten times his size. He'd doubled in bulk since I adopted him, and was a terrible food scavenger. To my delight, since the first day he climbed into my lap, shaking, at the pound, he'd been my biggest fan, my stout defender, and my reliable snuggle partner. Now, once Bethany scratched his head and got a few licks, he shook himself and waddled over to a tree stump to relieve himself.

"The woman who came by today? I've never met her, and she wouldn't leave a name. But she was practically apoplectic." I smiled; even though "practically apoplectic" didn't sound promising, I did love Bethany's vocabulary. "She told me she absolutely needed to talk to you."

"Well, I'm here now," I said. "She can come find me."

"Right," Bethany said, but a cloud had passed over her bright face.

"What's wrong?" I asked.

"She said something about you stealing the store."

"Stealing the store?"

She shrugged. "I don't know what she meant. But I got the impression she's planning to instigate trouble."

"Fabulous," I said. "Well, what's a good story without a few plot twists?" This was part of my new goal, which was to look on the bright side and count my blessings. Some days were easier than others. "Speaking of stories, how's your mystery going?" I asked.

"I've gotten to the dead body," she said, "but now I'm kind of stuck. I put the book to the side until after the grand re-opening, though. I've got K.T. Anderson set up for a reading an hour after it starts, and I even talked the local paper into sending a reporter over tomorrow!"

K.T. Anderson was a Maine-based bestselling mystery author who had set an entire series in a town not far from here; getting her to come to the grand opening was a coup. "You are amazing, Bethany," I said, meaning every word.

"Happy to do it. Come see what I've done!"

Leaving my U-Haul trailer behind and feeling rather brighter, I followed my young assistant into Seaside Cottage Books, Winston trotting along at my heels.

The bright blue walls and white bookshelves were fresh and clean, the neatly stacked books like jewels just waiting to be plucked from the shelves. The window seat in the bay window at the front of the store was lined with my handmade pillows, an inviting nook to tuck into with a book, and the armchairs tucked into the corners here and there gave the whole place the sweet, cozy feel I remembered from when I'd spent summer afternoons in the shop as a girl, when Loretta was still in good health. I walked from room to room, the gleaming wood floors creaking under my feet, and resisted the urge to pinch myself. Where the store had been dark and close, the windows covered over with old blankets and the rooms smelling of dust and must when I first took possession, over the past few months, Bethany and I had transformed it into a bright, clean space that smelled of lemon and new books and, above all, possibility.

"I set the table up here in the room with the local books, under the window," Bethany said, leading me to one of the front rooms. "I'm featuring K.T. Anderson's latest, of course. I didn't like it as much as the last one—it's a little heavy on the romance part—but it'll sell well. I ordered lots of stock for her to sign." Sure enough, a table with a bright blue tablecloth sat along the wall, two coffee percolators and several platters waiting for the cookies I'd been stocking the freezer with for the last month. A stack of postcards was displayed prominently on shelves and tables around the store that showed a picture of Seaside Books, including a 10% off coupon and the promo copy we'd come up with together—"Sink Your Teeth into a Good Book--Free Cookie with Every Purchase."

"It looks terrific," I said. "I don't know how I'll ever thank you."

"Become a booming success and feature my first book," Bethany said, "and we'll call it even."

"Of course," I said, grinning at her. I had total faith in Bethany; she was smart, enthusiastic, dedicated, and one of the hardest workers I knew.

I glanced around the store, which was picture-perfect and ready for opening, with pride and anticipation mixed with a little bit of anxiety. After all, everything was riding on this venture. I'd spent the last twenty years taking care of my daughters, running a home, and working part-time at one of Boston's independent bookstores, Bean Books. Now that I was single again, I needed to be able to take care of myself, and after being out of the workforce for two decades, my prospects in corporate America were rather limited. Besides, I couldn't envision spending the next twenty years in some oatmeal-colored cubicle answering phones and doing filing, which was pretty much the only option available for someone with my work experience.

Although Ellie, the owner of Bean Books and a dear friend, had offered me an assistant manager position, with real estate prices in Boston, there was no way I could pay my rent with the salary she was able to offer me. When Ellie told me Loretta was ill and might be looking for someone to help run Seaside Cottage Books—or even take it over for her—something inside me responded. I'd always fantasized about owning my own bookstore and living in a small community, and I wasn't getting any younger. Did I really want "She always wanted to own a bookstore but never got around to it" in my obituary? No matter what happened, I was glad I'd gone after what I'd always wanted; and Ellie had been a terrific cheerleader and consultant during my moments of doubt.

Winston seemed to approve of the new digs, too; he'd settled down into the dog bed I'd put beside the old desk I was using as a counter, looking content for the first time that day. Or at least relieved to be out of his crate. I knew the demand for dinner would be coming soon, though.

"Mail is in the top drawer of the desk—there were a few things that looked important, so I put them on top of the stack—and I shelved another order of books that came in today," Bethany informed me. "There was a new one from

Barbara Ross in the order, so I put it in the New Releases display."

"Perfect," I told her.

"I'm going to head home for dinner," she said. "But I'll be back tomorrow. If you need help unloading, I can ask my cousins to come give us a hand tomorrow morning."

"That would be a massive help; there's no way I could get that couch up the stairs on my own, much less the mattress. I can't thank you enough!"

"See you in the morning, then. I can't wait!"

"Text me when you get home, okay?'

"I will," she promised.

I watched through the front window as Bethany climbed onto her bike and turned right on Cottage Street, keeping my eyes on her until she disappeared from sight. Her house was only a few blocks away. I knew Snug Harbor was safe, but I also knew I wouldn't sleep soundly unless I knew Bethany had gotten home okay.

Once a mother, always a mother, I suppose.

∼

"Let's stretch our legs," I suggested, grabbing a leash from the passenger seat of the car and clipping it to Winston's collar. With a glance back at the house—and the U-Haul I still had to unload — we headed down the grassy trail to the water, pausing to inspect a few raspberry bushes with berries hidden under the yellow-green leaves, Winston straining at the leash and sniffing everything in range. Berries I would pick and put into ice cream sundaes, into muffins... I had so many things to look forward to this summer. Beach roses filled the air with their winey perfume, the bright blooms studding the dark green foliage.

Winston romped happily toward the water, smelling all the grass tufts, only slowing down and treading carefully when we got to the rocky beach. The tide was halfway out, and Winston was staying close beside me. Even though the waves in the harbor were minimal, he'd been swamped by a rogue wave once, and had had new respect for the ocean ever since. As we walked, I scanned the dark rocks mixed with flecks of brown seaweed, searching out of habit for sea glass. I found two brown chunks, doubtless the remains of old beer bottles, a couple of green shards, and two bits of delicate pale green that must have started life as Coke bottles, and I was about to turn back when a glint of cobalt caught my eye. I scooped it up and rinsed it off; it was a beautiful, deep blue shard, my favorite color and a lucky find. I tucked it in my pocket and walked up the beach, my stomach rumbling. What I really wanted to do was go to one of those restaurants up the street and indulge in a lobster dinner, but I was on a tunafish budget, so a homemade sandwich would have to do.

I grabbed the overnight case from the back seat of the SUV and climbed the back stairs to the apartment porch, Winston in my wake. Then I unlocked the door and stepped inside, flipping on the light with my elbow, and smiled. It was cozy, sweet, and... in a word, perfect.

In the back of the little house, with a gorgeous view of the harbor, was the living room, whose natural-colored floors and white walls (I'd painted) looked fresh and bright, even in the evening. Although the furnishings currently consisted of a rag rug, two folding chairs, and a dust mop, I could picture how it would be once I brought in my white couch and coffee table, with a big blue rag rug against the golden floor.

The kitchen was small, but cozy, also with wood floors

and white walls, with a card table I'd gotten at the secondhand store in the corner. I'd outfitted the kitchen with odds and ends from my kitchen in Boston, including a toaster I'd been meaning to throw away for years, a coffeemaker that had been state-of-the-art in the late 1990s, and stacks of white and blue plates from Goodwill. I plopped down my overnight bag, released Winston from his leash, and grabbed a loaf of bread I'd put in the freezer the last time I was here, tucking two slices into the toaster oven and fishing in the small fridge for cheese. A bottle of cheap but not entirely undrinkable Prosecco sat in the fridge door; I'd bought it in anticipation of this night.

I slapped a slice of cheddar cheese on each piece of bread, then hit "toast" and retrieved a jam jar from the cabinet. While Winston watched, I popped the cork on the Prosecco and filled the jar. Then, jam jar in hand, I walked into the living room and surveyed the view from the kitchen window, which overlooked the harbor.

The sandbar connecting Snug Harbor to Snug Island had almost been swallowed up by the tide, and two late seagulls picked through the broken shells at the water's edge. Two sea kayakers were heading out from the island, paddling toward Snug Harbor, probably anxious to get back before total darkness fell. The sky was rose and peach and deep, deep, blue, and the first two stars twinkled in the cobalt swath of sky.

I looked down to where Winston stood behind me, looking up at me expectantly, head cocked to one side. "To new beginnings," I said, slipping my companion a piece of cheese before raising my jar in a toast, then sipping the fizzy Prosecco. "We made it."

As I spoke, I noticed a furtive figure slipping out of the trees and creeping up the path to the house. Then it paused, and I could see the pale oval of a face looking up at the lit window. As if whoever it was had changed their mind, he or she hustled back into the trees, melting into the shadows. Beside me, standing at the glass door, Winston's hackles rose, and he growled.

Goose bumps rose on my arms for the second time that night—this time, not in a good way. "It's okay," I reassured the little dog, hoping to reassure myself at the same time. "Whoever it is is gone."

As I spoke, the smell of burning toast filled the air. "Drat," I said, and hurried back to the kitchen, where the edges of the toast had blackened.

I pulled it out of the toaster and onto a plate, burning myself in the process, and cut off the edges with a butter knife, then sat down at the table with my sad-looking toasted cheese sandwich and a jam jar of Prosecco, still wondering who had headed up the path and changed tacks at the last minute.

Whoever it was was gone, I told myself as I bit into my sandwich. And I had other things to worry about.

Like unpacking the truck.

And preparing to have all of Snug Harbor descend on my fledgling bookstore in less than 24 hours.

∼

It was almost midnight by the time I tucked in with Winston curled up in the crook of my arm. I hoped it was my last night sleeping on an air mattress, but with my crisp blue and white percale sheets, fluffy blanket, and soft pillows, it wasn't exactly a hardship. Besides, it was lovely being able to see the stars out my window; and to open my window and hear the lap of the water against the shore and the breeze in the maple tree next to the house instead of Boston traffic in the distance.

I read one of Lee Strauss's charming Ginger Gold books until my eyes started to droop. Then I reached to turn off the lamp I'd set up next to the head of the mattress and burrowed into the covers, lulled to sleep by Winston's steady breathing and the soothing sound of the ocean.

Until a crashing sound from downstairs woke me up.

A Killer Ending will be out this June... pre-order your copy here to find out what happens next!

RECIPES

APPLE COFFEE CAKE

Ingredients:

Cake

1/4 cup butter, softened
3/4 cup brown sugar
1 large egg
1/2 cup sour cream
1 1/2 teaspoon vanilla extract
1 cup all-purpose flour
3/4 teaspoon ground cinnamon
1/2 teaspoon baking soda
1/4 teaspoon salt
2 cups diced Honeycrisp or Granny Smith apple

Topping

1/4 cup brown sugar
1/4 cup all-purpose flour
2 tablespoons butter

1/2 teaspoon ground cinnamon

Instructions:

Preheat oven to 350 degrees F. Spray an 8-inch square baking dish with cooking spray; dust with 1 tablespoon flour.

Beat 1/4 cup butter and 3/4 cup brown sugar together with an electric mixer in a large bowl until light and fluffy. The mixture should be noticeably lighter in color. Beat egg into butter mixture. Add sour cream and vanilla extract to the mixture and beat in.

Stir 1 cup flour, 3/4 teaspoon cinnamon, baking soda, and salt together in a bowl; add to the butter mixture and beat to combine into a batter. Fold apples into the batter and pour into prepared baking dish.

Mix 1/4 cup brown sugar, 1/4 cup flour, 2 tablespoons butter, and 1/2 teaspoon cinnamon together in a bowl using a fork to achieve a crumbly consistency; sprinkle over the top of the batter.

Bake in the preheated oven until a toothpick inserted into the center comes out clean, 35 to 40 minutes. Cool in the pan for 10 minutes before removing to cool completely on a wire rack.

EASY THAI CURRY

Ingredients:

16 oz extra firm tofu

Optional Tofu Marinade

2 garlic cloves, minced
3 tbsp tamari or soy sauce
2 tbsp sesame oil
1 tbsp honey or brown sugar
3 tbsp rice vinegar
1 tsp red pepper flakes

Curry

1 yellow onion, finely chopped
3 garlic cloves, minced
1 tsp grated ginger
1 red, yellow, or orange bell pepper
1 cup thinly sliced mushrooms, preferably baby bella

3 tbsp red Thai curry paste
13 oz coconut milk
1 tbsp fish sauce (omit to make this dish vegetarian)
1 tbsp sambal oelek chili sauce
1 lime, zest and juice

Garnishes

Thai basil
Thinly sliced scallions

Instructions:

Tofu Marinade

Toss all of the marinade ingredients together in a large bowl. Put tofu in a large freezer bag or sealable container and pour the marinade over top. Refrigerate for 30-40 minutes.

Tofu

Drain tofu and seal in a plastic bag, then place the tofu in the freezer overnight. About 30 minutes before dinner, remove the tofu from the freezer and bring a pot of salted water to a boil. When the water is boiling, carefully submerge the tofu in the water and let it boil for 15 minutes. When done, carefully remove the tofu from the water with tongs and place on a plate or cutting board lined with paper towels. Lightly squeeze the block of tofu with paper towels to rid of excess water. Set aside to cool. (If you're marinating the tofu, do this about an hour before cooking to allow time for marinating.) Once the tofu has cooled, cut it into half-inch cubes.

Heat a large skillet over moderate heat and add a tablespoon of oil. Add the cubed tofu and sear for about five minutes on one side. After five minutes, or once the tofu has developed a golden crisp, carefully flip over and crisp up the other side and cook for another five minutes. When tofu is done, remove from heat, cover to keep warm, and set aside while you prepare the curry.

Curry

In a large saucepan bring 1/4 cup of water to a simmer over moderate heat. Add the minced onion, garlic, and fresh ginger. Stir to combine, and simmer for about 5 minutes or until the garlic is fragrant and the onions are translucent.

Add the sliced bell pepper and mushrooms, then add the red curry paste and stir until the vegetables are evenly coated.

Add the coconut milk, fish sauce, sambal oelek, lime juice, and lime zest. Stir until the curry paste has dissolved into the liquid and there are no clumps. Turn heat to low and let the curry simmer for 15 minutes.

Serve curry over rice. Top with crispy tofu and garnish with fresh Thai basil and sliced scallions.

GRAY WHALE INN BREAKFAST CASSEROLE

Ingredients:

1 pound mild ground pork sausage
1 pound hot ground pork sausage
1 (30-ounce) package frozen hash browns
1 1/2 teaspoons salt, divided
1/2 teaspoon pepper
1 cup shredded Cheddar cheese
6 large eggs
2 cups milk
Sliced avocado (optional)
Pico de gallo (optional)
Green onions (optional)
Sour cream (optional)

Instructions:

Preheat oven to 350°. Cook sausages in a large skillet over medium-high heat, stirring until sausage crumbles and is no longer pink. Drain well.

Prepare hash browns according to package directions, using 1/2 teaspoon salt and pepper. Stir together hash browns, sausage, and cheese, and pour into a lightly greased 13- x 9-inch baking dish.

Whisk together eggs, milk, and remaining 1 teaspoon salt. Pour evenly over potato mixture and bake for 35 to 40 minutes.

If desired, top with sliced avocados, pico de gallo, and a dollop of sour cream and sprinkle with green onions.

MAPLE WALNUT COFFEE CAKE

Ingredients:

Streusel:

1/2 cup light brown sugar
1/4 cup flour
1/4 cup finely chopped walnuts
1/2 teaspoon ground cinnamon
3 tablespoons unsalted butter, melted

Coffee Cake:

2 cups all-purpose flour
1 teaspoon baking powder
1/2 teaspoon baking soda
1/2 teaspoon fine salt
1/2 cup light brown sugar
1/2 cup chopped walnuts
1/2 cup maple syrup
1/2 cup vegetable oil

1/4 cup whole milk
2 large eggs, beaten
1 teaspoon maple extract
8 ounces sour cream

Topping:

1/2 cup powdered sugar
2 tablespoons maple syrup

Instructions:

Preheat the oven to 350°F. Spray the bottom of an 8-inch square pan with nonstick cooking spray.

Make the streusel:

In a small bowl, combine all of the streusel ingredients with a fork until crumbly.

Make the cake:

In a large bowl, stir together the flour, baking powder, baking soda, salt, brown sugar, and walnuts. In a small bowl, combine the maple syrup, oil, milk, eggs, and maple extract, then stir in the sour cream. Make a well in the center of the dry ingredients, then pour in the wet ingredients. Stir gently, until just combined.

Spoon half of the batter into the prepared pan, then sprinkle with half of the streusel. Spread the remaining batter over the streusel; sprinkle with the remaining streusel.

Bake for 35 minutes, or until a toothpick inserted in the center comes out clean. Cool for 15-20 minutes.

Make the topping:

In a small bowl, combine the sugar and maple syrup until a thick, pourable icing forms. Drizzle over the warm cake.

Cut into squares and serve.

SUGAR-TOPPED CRANBERRY MUFFINS

Ingredients:

2 cups all-purpose flour
3/4 cup packed brown sugar
2 teaspoons baking powder
2 large eggs
2/3 cup orange juice
1/3 cup melted butter
1 cup cranberries, coarsely chopped
1 cup chopped walnuts
Turbinado sugar (for sprinkling)

Instructions:

Preheat oven to 375° and line 12 muffin cups. In a large bowl, combine flour, brown sugar and baking powder.

In a medium-size bowl, beat eggs, then add orange juice and melted butter. Stir egg mixture into dry ingredients just until moistened (batter will be lumpy).

Fold in cranberries and walnuts and spoon into lined muffin cups. Sprinkle tops with turbinado sugar. Bake for 20 minutes or until golden brown; remove muffins from pan to cool on a wire rack.

FUDGY BUNDT CAKE

INGREDIENTS:

Cake

1 cup brewed coffee
1 cup unsalted butter
3/4 cup cocoa powder
2 cups sugar
3/4 teaspoon baking powder
1/4 teaspoon baking soda
3/4 teaspoon salt
2 cups flour
2 teaspoons vanilla extract
2 large eggs
1/2 cup sour cream

Icing

2/3 cup bittersweet chocolate chips
1/4 cup heavy whipping cream

INSTRUCTIONS:

Cake

Preheat the oven to 350°F.

Add the coffee, butter, and cocoa to a small saucepan and heat, stirring, until the butter melts. Remove from the heat and whisk until smooth, then let the mixture cool for 10 minutes.

While the chocolate is cooling, place the sugar, baking powder, baking soda, salt, and flour into a mixing bowl; whisk to combine.

When the chocolate mixture has cooled, add it to the bowl with the dry ingredients and mix until thoroughly combined, being sure to scrape the bottom and sides of the bowl.

In a medium bowl, whisk together the vanilla, eggs, and sour cream or yogurt. Stir into the chocolate batter, mixing until thoroughly combined.

Thoroughly grease a 10- to 12-cup Bundt pan (preferably non-stick) and pour the batter into the prepared pan. Bake the cake for 50 to 55 minutes, until a toothpick or skewer inserted into the center comes out clean. (If your pan has a dark interior, start checking at 40 minutes.)

Remove the cake from the oven, wait 5 minutes, and turn the pan over onto a cooling rack. Wait 5 more minutes, then lift the pan off the cake. Let the cake cool completely before icing.

Icing

Add the chocolate and cream to a microwave-safe bowl, or in a saucepan set over medium heat. Heat until the cream starts to bubble around the edges (watch carefully so it doesn't burn).

Remove icing from heat stir until the chocolate melts and the mixture is smooth. Spoon the icing over the top of the cooled cake, letting it drip down the sides.

MORE BOOKS BY KAREN MACINERNEY

To download a free book and receive members-only outtakes, giveaways, short stories, recipes, and updates, join Karen's Reader's Circle at www.karenmacinerney.com! You can also join her Facebook community; she often hosts giveaways and loves getting to know her readers there.

And don't forget to follow her on BookBub to get newsflashes on new releases!

The Gray Whale Inn Mysteries
Murder on the Rocks
Dead and Berried
Murder Most Maine
Berried to the Hilt
Brush With Death
Death Runs Adrift
Whale of a Crime
Claws for Alarm
Scone Cold Dead
Anchored Inn

Cookbook: The Gray Whale Inn Kitchen
Four Seasons of Mystery (A Gray Whale Inn Collection)
Blueberry Blues (A Gray Whale Inn Short Story)
Pumpkin Pied (A Gray Whale Inn Short Story)
Iced Inn (A Gray Whale Inn Short Story)
Lupine Lies (A Gray Whale Inn Short Story)

The Snug Harbor Mysteries
A Killer Ending (June 2020)
Inked Out (Fall 2020)

The Dewberry Farm Mysteries
Killer Jam
Fatal Frost
Deadly Brew
Mistletoe Murder
Dyeing Season
Wicked Harvest
Sweet Revenge, Summer/Fall 2020
Cookbook: Lucy's Farmhouse Kitchen

The Margie Peterson Mysteries
Mother's Day Out
Mother Knows Best
Mother's Little Helper

Tales of an Urban Werewolf
Howling at the Moon
On the Prowl
Leader of the Pack

ACKNOWLEDGMENTS

First, many thanks to my family, not just for putting up with me, but for continuing to come up with creative ways to kill people. (You should see the looks we get in restaurants.) And thank you to Andy Krell for the plot ideas (and U-Boat research)!

Special thanks to my mother, Carol Swartz, for her constant encouragement and careful reading of the manuscript. (Thanks to my father, Dave Swartz, too... I saw your comments in there.) What would I do without you???

Thanks (as always) to Bob Dombrowski for his incredible artwork. Kim Killion, as always, did an amazing job putting together the cover design, and Angelika Offenwanger's sharp editorial eye helped keep me from embarrassing myself. Thank you also to Holly Duty for helping me with covers and much, much more.

And finally, thank you to ALL of the wonderful readers who

make Gray Whale Inn possible, especially my fabulous Facebook community. You keep me going!

ABOUT THE AUTHOR

Karen MacInerney is the *USA Today* bestselling author of multiple mystery series, and her victims number well into the double digits. She lives in Austin, Texas with her sassy family, Tristan, and Little Bit (a.k.a. Dog #1 and Dog #2).

Feel free to visit Karen's web site at www.karenmacinerney.com, where you can download a free book and sign up for her Readers' Circle to receive subscriber-only short stories, deleted scenes, recipes and other bonus material. You can also find her on Facebook (she spends an inordinate amount of time there), where Karen loves getting to know her readers, answering questions, and offering quirky, behind-the-scenes looks at the writing process (and life in general).

P. S. Don't forget to follow Karen on BookBub to get news-flashes on new releases!

www.karenmacinerney.com
karen@karenmacinerney.com

facebook.com/AuthorKarenMacInerney
twitter.com/KarenMacInerney

Printed in Great Britain
by Amazon